Grace Driven Life

By Beverly Angel

Published by: LEVI HOUSE

Unless otherwise stated, all scripture quotations are taken from the King James Version of the Bible.

ISBN **978-0-9957499-5-5**

Copyright 2018 by Beverly Angel

Published by LEVI HOUSE

Contents

Chapter One

Breaking the Magicians Code

We have all seen him

He first appeared on our television screens a dark shadowy figure draped in all black. Tall and intimidating, the very sight of him without a doubt made your heart palpitate with such force, you could feel the rush of blood rippling through your throbbing temples. Wearing a dark mask with strange claw-like markings, his red-rimmed eyes glaring menacingly from behind it added yet another layer of terror. When he announced himself to the viewers, his raspy voice was enough to immobilize us with fear. And at the sound of it, I felt my teenage legs lose their agility and crumble beneath me. It was just a show, but it was well presented. It was the Masked Magician's Breaking the Magician's Code.

The concept behind Breaking the Magician's Code was to reveal the secrets behind famous magic tricks. The job of the Masked Magician was simple but required both skill and security. He would arrest the attention of his viewing audience by performing large-scale illusions and a few smaller close-up magic tricks before revealing the secrets of the tricks. The Masked Magician was, in fact, a well-known magician who wore a mask to avoid recrimination from fellow magicians.

The Masked Magician's mask was not only for dramatic effect but also to protect his identity. Even his assistants were left unidentified and uncredited for security purposes. The Masked Magician faced some backlash from some fellow magicians who believed his illusion-spoiling acts were a betrayal of their profession. As a matter of fact, a coalition of magicians' groups organized free magic shows and urged a viewer boycott of Breaking the Magician's Code as revenge for the discrediting of their craft. Yet, the show continued for more seasons. What kept viewers watching? People could not resist the Masked Magician's act.

The Works Code

Each time the Masked Magician performed an act, he and his assistants would take us behind the scenes to reveal what was really going on. Behind each seemingly complicated and mesmerizing performance was a very simple sleight of hand technique that the eye of the viewer was just too slow to catch. It was a revelation of very sophisticated trickery. The ultimate reveal came during the final show of the series when the Masked Magician removed his mask and showed the world his true identity. The whole world to their dismay finally realized that the huge towering intimidating figure was just an average slightly built middle-aged man who looked like he could barely mash an ant. The mask, clothing, and masterful manipulation of lighting and camera angles had made the Masked Magician appear larger than life.

A similar form of trickery exists in the Church today. There has been a wrong gospel propagated in the Church. It is a works driven movement that is promoted with the speed of slick speech and forced camera angles with distorted perspectives in a "magic show" that has hidden the real Gospel behind the mask of works-based religion. Just like magicians pretend to be able to do something that their audience can't do, these sleight of hand preachers peer out from behind strange masks demanding works that they themselves can't do. Even Jesus exposed this problem and shouted (Matthew 23:3-4):

For they preach but do not practise. They pile up back-breaking burdens and lay them on other men's shoulders—yet they themselves will not raise a finger to move them.

It is a works driven life instead of a grace driven life that has stolen the Church's eyes and attention, and many believers are busy watching the hand but not noticing the sleight!

Sleight of Hand

The word sleight refers to cunning or craft used in deceiving. Sleight of hand trickery is the art of mastering distraction for the purpose of deception. A sleight of hand magician employs the skilful use of hand methods and finger techniques to entertain or manipulate (also known as prestidigitation or legerdemain). Some of these magicians are expert enough to be within a few feet of an audience and pull off magic tricks, card cheating, card flourishing, or stealing. If the sleight is well-performed, it will look like a completely natural innocent gesture or change in hand-position or body posture. Manual dexterity is not the only thing involved in sleight of hand. It also relies heavily on the use of psychology, timing, and a balance of misdirected focus and distraction in accomplishing a magical effect. This is what the Church has become with its insistence on the 'works driven life.'

Stay with me as I delve a little deeper. Experts have discovered that the brain has two kinds of attention. The first, called "top-down" or decision-making attention, is what you use when you decide to focus on a stimulus or task. Second, we employ "bottom-up" or surprise attention which happens when we quickly shift our focus onto an unexpected stimulus, such as a ringing phone. Magicians trick you by occupying both forms of your attention. Left with no others, you're completely and hopelessly distracted from their sleights of hand. In short, our brains only allow us to concentrate on one thing at a time. This is why we are highly susceptible to sleight of hand trickery. Magicians utilize people's inherent single-mindedness to their advantage. And there are many preachers who utilize it to great effect as well.

Do you realise?

Do you realise that many believers have been subjected to religion's sleight of hand, and they suffer because of it? Perhaps you're one of them. They suffer because of preachers and leaders who are trained in preaching tactics, methodologies, and doctrines that promote the reliance on self-effort and performance as a way to be approved by God or appease Him. Much like the masterful positioning of lights and camera angles to create an intended illusion, this works-based message is cunningly crafted to entice the believer to rely on his or her own works rather than on the grace freely given by Christ.

Let's pursue this point a little further and hear from someone who was skilled in sleight of hand. Apollo Robbins is an expert sleight of hand artist. He is described as "an artful manipulator of awareness." It has been said that among his peers, he is widely considered the best in the world at what he does, which is taking things from people's jackets, pants, purses, wrists, fingers, and necks, then returning them in amusing and mind-boggling ways. He gained notoriety after pickpocketing Secret Service agents accompanying Jimmy Carter, former US President. He successfully stole, among other items, President Carter's itinerary and the keys to his motorcade. When asked how he was able to manage such remarkable feats Robbins said, "Distracting people can be quite simple!"

Robbins employed "top-down distractions" by getting people to focus either on a conversation or on his actions. By being entertaining or just confusing, he commanded their attention. Meanwhile, on the side, he quietly removed their belongings. Expounding on his technique, Robbins said, "If I need to steal from a difficult spot, I like to use a 'bottom-up' attention strategy to direct the focus." Clapping loudly, a sudden movement, or in an example demonstrated in the show, waving a spoon in the air, are all examples of such strategies. You might think that you, unlike most other people, wouldn't fall for such simple strategies. You think because you're a multi-tasker you can pay close attention to several things at once. But to think so would be a mistake.

There is a myth that has been perpetuated. It's called multi-tasking. The truth is that our brains are programmed to concentrate on one thing at a time. There are many people who believe they are able to do multiple things at the same time. They call it multi-tasking. However, according to experts, multi-tasking is an illusion. What most people call multi-tasking is really multi-switching. Remember, the brain can only focus on one thing at a time. So, when people think they are multi-tasking, they are really multi-switching. That is to say, they are simply switching from one activity to another. You may have the illusion that you are balancing all your tasks equally and performing well at all of them. In reality, this illusion causes you to become blind to your own impaired performance.

The sleight of hand magician takes advantage of this inability to multi-task. One of the ways a sleight of hand magician is able to create an effective illusion is to direct the focus on a particular action. Then while he has your attention focused on one thing, he does another. When watching an expert magician make a playing card vanish, pick-pocket a volunteer, or perform any other startling sleight of hand trick, it seems that the harder you try to pay attention to what the magician is doing, the more easily you're fooled. This is why it's so frustrating when you fail to catch a magician in their act. You can't help but wonder, how did they manage to trick you. The same happens when the believer awakes from the works driven life and embraces the grace driven life. They can't help but wonder why they didn't see the dangers of the works driven life. This misdirected focus on works driven living has entered the Church in full force. Believers are being hoodwinked and fleeced through a religious sleight of hand!

In fact, when the apostle Paul saw the Galatians falling into the same trap he called it witchcraft. Watch what the Bible says:

Galatians 3:1-3
O foolish Galatians, who hath bewitched you, that ye should not obey the truth, before whose eyes Jesus Christ hath been evidently set forth, crucified among you? This only would I learn of you, received ye the Spirit by works of the law, or by the hearing of faith? Are ye so foolish? Having begun in the Spirit, are ye now made perfect by the flesh?

The Galatians had fallen into the same trap trying to do for themselves what God had already completed in Christ. It was as if someone had cast a spell on them and deceived them into working for what they already possessed.

Spiritual Scooby-Doo

There was an animated TV show introduced in the late 60s called Scooby-Doo, Where Are You? In each episode, Scooby-Doo, a Great Dane, joins four California high school students (Fred, Daphne, Velma and Shaggy) on a quest to solve strange mysteries (usually involving a ghost or some other monstrous creature). Scooby-Doo was as big as a lion, but he had the heart of a mouse! For most of the show, Scooby-Doo would run around cowering in fear trying to hide behind someone or something often much smaller than he was. He feared a ghost that never really existed. But Scooby would see the strange apparition and experience the fear as if it were real. Invariably, the ghost (or monster) was apprehended and revealed to be a relatively innocuous individual who used the disguise to cover up some wrongdoing. The villain would almost always exclaim "And I would have gotten away with it too if it weren't for you meddling kids!"

I'll close this chapter by asking the same question that was asked of Scooby-Doo. Where are you? Have you, like Scooby, been duped into believing something to be true that is merely a well-rigged works-based illusion? If that is so, we don't intend to let the villains get away with it. We are here to break the magician's code by revealing the tricks that have been used to create a lifestyle based on fear instead of a lifestyle based on grace. We are ripping off the mask so that you can see what's really behind this false doctrine. This book is written so that, no matter how well presented, no sleight of hand religious "magician" will ever be able to deceive you into believing that you have to work to earn God's approval. Stay with me as in each chapter I delve a little deeper into the wonderful discovery of the grace driven life.

Chapter Two

Righteousness Is A Gift Not A Reward

There are so many believers in the Church today who have been hoodwinked into believing that God demands that they do right for them to make it to Heaven. You do not need to live right to go to Heaven. Yes, you heard me correctly. In fact, you are the very reason I am writing this book. Without even realizing it, this "live right" way of thinking causes you to become more sin conscious than righteousness conscious. You might be wondering, what does it mean to be sin conscious? When you're sin conscious, you become so obsessed with trying not to sin that you end up doing the very thing you're trying to avoid. Let me explain it this way.

Have you ever noticed that when you drive a car, you steer in the direction of your focus? You might be determined to stay on course, but if your eyes look to the right, you will undoubtedly steer to the right even if that's not where you want to go. That's exactly what happens when you focus on works rather than righteousness. When you are trying to "live right," your focus is really set on the sin you're trying to avoid. Consequently, you inadvertently steer your life towards sin because that is where your focus is.

I want you to think about this very carefully because what you choose to focus on will ultimately determine what you become. Watch what the scripture says in 2 Corinthians:

2 Corinthians 3:18
But we all, with open face beholding as in a glass the glory of the Lord, are changed into the same image from glory to glory, even as by the Spirit of the Lord.

Paul was literally telling us in that verse that you become what you behold and what you focus on. It's a spiritual law. When God wants to heal you, He sends His word that proclaims your healing, and when you receive it and maintain your focus, your body has no choice but to be completely healed. When the enemy wants to keep you in bondage to sin, he only needs to employ one strategy, keep your focus on sin. And guess what, once you fall for it he can keep you there as long as he likes. But when you focus on righteousness, you are no longer trying to live right. Your focus is on the benefits that righteousness produces which in turn produces right living. As a result, your life is steered on a course of grace that leads to blessings and victory every time!

A Thimble or a Siphon

Now, I know when I mention the word righteousness many are already disqualifying themselves from the benefits of righteousness because they believe they are not quite there. In fact, this epidemic has so infected the Church today that those who are bold in their faith are actually accused of being pompous or show-offs.

God's people are being robbed and hoodwinked by preachers who seem to be advocating and teaching the righteousness of Christ. Yet in reality, they are actually advancing the enemy's agenda in the life of believers. Sin consciousness will rob you of the peace and joy that Christ purchased for you. The level of joy and victory in your life as a believer is directly proportional to the abundance of grace which you receive.

Some have taken more grace than others. If grace was likened to an endless ocean, there are some who only receive a thimbleful of grace; others receive buckets or barrels or tankers full of grace; some never even visit the ocean of grace. Then there are those who receive what the Bible refers to as "abundance of grace." We find this in the first part of Romans 5:17 where it says:

Romans 5:17
For if by one man's offence death reigned by one, much more they which receive abundance of grace and of the gift of righteousness shall reign in life by one, Jesus Christ.

Now when we talk about those which receive abundance of grace, these are the ones who employ what I call spiritual engineering, whereby they use the syphon of righteousness to tap into the never-ending flow of grace! These are the ones who reign as kings in this life. Why are some Christians failing while others are reigning? It is because they don't understand the gift of righteousness. Let's look at that scripture once more:

Romans 5:17
For if by one man's offence death reigned by one, much more they which receive abundance of grace and of the gift of righteousness shall reign in life by one, Jesus Christ.

Paul refers to those who receive abundance of grace. The Greek word translated as receive in that passage is lambano. It literally means to take a hold of, or to take in order to carry away. In other words, we could read this scripture as, they that take a hold of abundance of grace and of the of the gift of righteousness shall reign in life. Are you seeing this?

This thing we call grace is there for the taking brothers and sisters. In fact, I need to stay here until the penny drops. What Paul is talking about there is a breed of believers that have not been fooled by the sleight of hand in the Church today and have gotten a hold of what God has done for us.

When you read the scripture, you can actually tell that this was something that was close to the heart of the apostle Paul in his writings. And, when you examine that passage we have just read in the book of Romans, it's even clearer. Watch what the scripture says:

Romans 5:17
For if by one man's offence death reigned by one, much more they which receive abundance of grace and of the gift of righteousness shall reign in life by one, Jesus Christ.

The man is talking about those who take hold of the grace of God. One thing you always need to remember as a student of the Word is that the Bible does not just pile up words for no good reason. Every word you find in that passage is pointing to a certain truth that you need to get a hold of.

God was very specific about the level of grace you were meant to get a hold of. That word translated as abundance in that passage is perisseia. Now this is a word that the Greeks would use when they wanted to describe the excess wax in one's ears. So, when Paul talks about the abundance of grace right there, he is painting a picture of getting a hold of an overflowing grace, and he paints the picture so graphically for us right there.

Brothers and sisters, God wants you to take full advantage of the grace which is in Christ Jesus. How much grace do you want? There is grace for anything and everything. Grace is that overflowing of God's ability in your life. Grace is that glory of God working for you. Everything that God gives to you comes through grace. God has already provided abundant grace in Christ; all you must do is take a hold of it. But, if you want to reign as a king in this life, you must also make full use of the gift of righteousness. Therefore, it behoves us to take a closer look at what righteousness is all about.

Righteousness is of the Spirit

Now, as plainly as it is written in that passage of scripture we have just read it is still a very difficult thing for the religious mind to accept that the Christian has received righteousness as a gift. I know I have some witnesses reading this right now. Anyway, I did not mention your name so let's move on.

When the Bible says gift of righteousness, it actually means just that—it's a gift. There is no other super spiritual meaning behind it. Just so I know we are on the same page here, if you went to work for a month, the pay cheque you receive is not a gift but a wage. In other words, you earned it, you deserved it. But when you wake up on Christmas morning and find that brand new laptop you have been obsessing about under the tree, that's a gift. Someone just bought it for you because they knew it would make you happy.

Romans 5:17
For if by one man's offence death reigned by one, much more they which receive abundance of grace and of the gift of righteousness shall reign in life by one, Jesus Christ.

So then, what is righteousness? Righteousness refers to several things. First, it means the rightness of God. It is the nature of God to be right only. God cannot be wrong. It is impossible for Him to be wrong. He is the reference for righteousness. When you look in the dictionary under righteousness, it should say, see God. He is the standard for deciding rightness. That's wonderful! But, here's something that's even more exciting.

That nature and ability to be right and right only which no one else could ever have but God, God gave it to you as a gift. And because you have that gift of righteousness, you are awakened to something that this righteousness produces. It produces what is called right standing. That is the ability to stand in the presence of God—the most righteous Person—without a sense of guilt, condemnation, or inferiority. That's a result of righteousness.

You are not afraid of God because you have His nature of rightness which has been imparted to your spirit. It's His gift imparted to you. If it were possible for you to obey all the laws of God, you could come to God and say that you are qualified, but you couldn't. That failure to qualify is what causes you to become afraid of God as Adam did when he fell into sin (see Genesis 3:8-15). But, because of the gift of righteousness, you can stand before God without fear.

God did not just give you a portion of righteousness. He gave you all of it. Righteousness is an impartation into your spirit. It is His righteousness, all of it, imparted to your spirit. It doesn't grow. You cannot be more righteous than you are right now no matter what you do or do not do.

Let me shock you even further. No believer is more righteous than any other believer. We have all received the same gift of righteousness, and no one can be righteous without it. Picture for a moment that great man or woman of God you admire and respect. You think they are more righteous than you are and that's why they can do mighty works, but nothing could be further from the truth. They are just as righteous as you are. The problem is you have been focusing on trying not to sin instead of reaping the benefits of the gift of righteousness you have. It's already all there.

What you need is a consciousness of this righteousness more than consciousness of sin. Recognize it as real, recognize it as being present, then walk in the light of it. Now, fasten your seatbelt and get ready because when you catch the revelation of what I'm about to say, it will change everything! Are you ready for it? Here it is. You are as righteous as Jesus is righteous because it is His righteousness that has been given to you as a gift! Take a moment and let that soak in. You are as righteous as Jesus is righteous!

I know I just killed a religious demon right there! Remember whose righteousness you are receiving as a gift. I can already imagine some of you saying, hold on a minute! How can I be as righteous as Jesus is righteous? I mess up. I don't always act right, talk right, or think right. I don't feel righteous, sometimes I don't even look righteous. All of that may be the facts, but here's the truth: God loves you independent of your performance. He isn't dealing with us based on our actions or even our thoughts. He is dealing with us based on our spirits which have been made new and into which righteousness has been imparted. Understanding this motivates us to serve God out of love instead of serving God out of fear that we're going to be punished, rejected, or that our prayers won't be answered.

There is a song that I used to hear growing up that is still commonly sung in some church circles. It refers to the transformation of a believer after salvation. It goes something like this, "I looked at my hands, my hands looked new. I looked at my feet, and they did too." This song and the thinking behind it is a lie. The transformation that took place in you when you became a believer was not about your body or even your soul (mind, will, or emotions). It was your spirit that was made new. So, when you look in the mirror and think, "My thoughts weren't right." or "I don't feel right." or "I didn't do right." you have missed the point. God is not looking at any of that. He is looking at your spirit. That is what has been made new and that is where the gift of righteousness has been imparted. God is Spirit. Therefore, He sees your spirit and relates to your spirit. And even when you sin, fall short, or mess up, God does not change in His attitude toward you because He is looking at you and dealing with you in the spirit.

Righteousness Was Here Before You Were

Understand that God is not a reactive God. He is a proactive God. The Bible says of Him that He declares the end from the beginning:

Isaiah 46:10
Declaring the end from the beginning, and from ancient times the things that are not yet done, saying, My counsel shall stand, and I will do all my pleasure.

So, we are talking about a God who establishes the end and then works His way back to the beginning. He anticipates the need and then makes provision for it before you even realize that the need exists. As a matter of fact, He does this before you even exist. It has been this way from the beginning. God anticipated the needs of Adam and Eve, and before they ever existed, He created everything they'd ever need. When Adam and Eve needed something, they didn't have to go to God and ask for it. He had already created it. They didn't get hungry and then have to go to God for Him to provide food. Food was already there. They didn't say, I need to breathe, and God then created air. The air was waiting for them when they got there. He anticipated everything they would need. Follow me closely. I'm going somewhere.

In the beginning when God created food, He created more than enough, not just for Adam and Eve, but for all seven billion of us and however many more will come after us. When He created oxygen, He created enough for everybody who will ever come into existence. Mankind entered into this completion that God had created. That blessing and benefit was not just for Adam and Eve. It was for you too! God has also anticipated everything that you need. Understand that God is not creating anything. He created in the beginning, and then He rested from His work. Watch what the scripture says in Genesis:

Genesis 2:2
And on the seventh day God ended His work which He had made; and He rested on the seventh day from all His work which He had made.

When the Bible says that God ended His work, it means that he ceased from what he had started. His work was done, He was not taking a holiday.

I want you to get this revelation. There is no more work to be done in order for you to be righteous. God has already given you everything you need to be righteous. Righteousness is a spiritual blessing, and according to Ephesians 1:3-4 you already have it. Let's look at it together:

Ephesians 1:3
Blessed be the God and Father of our Lord Jesus Christ, who hath blessed us with all spiritual blessings in heavenly places in Christ:

I know this might be hard for you to wrap your mind around, but you can't get God to give you any more blessings than He has already given you. The verse says He hath given us all spiritual blessings. That's past tense. In other words, it's a done deal. You are not going to be blessed. He's already done it! I don't know what all means where you come from, but where I come from all means all! God has already blessed you with all spiritual blessings. That's everything!

You can't get God to bless you any more than you've already been blessed. But, what you can do is to walk in more of the blessings of God and learn how to receive and appropriate what God has already done. This will become even clearer as we read on. Verse 4 says:

Ephesians 1:4
According as He hath chosen us in Him before the foundation of the world, that we should be holy and without blame before Him in love:

God did all this before the foundation of the world. That is amazing! Whatever age you are, I guarantee you're not older than the foundation of the world. Which simply means, this is not God responding or reacting to you or anything you do. This is God anticipating what you needed even before you existed and meeting that need in advance. If God would do this for food and air and everything else, why then do you think when it comes to righteousness that He would expect you to work for it?

You've Already Got It So Stop Trying to Get It!

Righteousness is not a reward for your good works. It is a spiritual blessing that God anticipated and for which He made provision before you ever came on the scene. Let's go a little further in that same chapter.

Ephesians 1:5-6
Having predestined us to adoption as sons by Jesus Christ to Himself, according to the good pleasure of His will, to the praise of the glory of His grace, by which He made us accepted in the Beloved.

Did you see that? You are already accepted! You are already loved! You don't have to work for it! It's not a reward for anything you did. It's grace! How many people are fighting and struggling and trying to earn acceptance with God? You're accepted in the Beloved before you were ever born! God the Father accepted Jesus, and any person who chooses to make Jesus his or her Lord is accepted in the Beloved. Why did He do it? It's right there in verse 5. He did it because He is good! Don't you see?

What God does for you is not based on what you do, it's based on His own nature, His own goodness, His own love. God loves you! He loves you just as much as He loves Jesus. He's just as pleased with you as He is with Jesus. Hallelujah! This is why you never have to worry that you're not good enough, not perfect enough, not sinless enough to be in right standing with God. You need only to believe that everything you need to be righteous was anticipated by God from the very beginning and has already been provided for you in and through Jesus Christ.

Did you know that the word for accepted in Ephesians 1:6 is only used twice in the scriptures? The only other place it was used is in Luke 1:28 where Mary is greeted by the angel and told that she was "highly favoured." It's the same word. To be accepted is to be highly favoured.

The reason Mary was highly favoured, contrary to what the magicians of our pulpits have told us, is not that she was the best and most deserving young woman in the village, oh no. It's actually the opposite. Now think about this for a moment. If I gave you a salary after a long day's work, yes you would be grateful, but that's not favour because you deserved it, you worked. But, if I came to you and just handed you $10000 for no apparent reason, that is favour, you did not deserve it. So, when Mary says that she is highly favoured, she is actually telling you that she was highly undeserving.

It's so wonderful to know that God has highly favoured you and you don't have to do a thing to earn that favour. Just accept that you are accepted. The Bible tells us that the wages of sin is death; but the gift of God is eternal life:

Romans 6:23
For the wages of sin is death; but the gift of God is eternal life through Jesus Christ our Lord.

The same way that you receive eternal life for your salvation, accept that righteousness is granted. You're as righteous as Christ. Righteousness is a gift. The only qualification for receiving it is for you to believe in Jesus Christ as the Son of the living God and confess that He is Lord of your life. Is righteousness just about God being right? No! It's more than that!

Righteousness Produces Right Living

The righteousness of God is about the goodness of God. Goodness is about righteousness, right judgment, deciding what is right from what is wrong. When you walk in the righteousness of God, you no longer concern yourself with who's right and who's wrong. There is an expression that refers to "looking at the world through rose coloured glasses" meaning such a person is always seeing the brighter or favourable view of things. Well, we have something better than rose coloured glasses. We have the righteousness of God which allows us to see the world and ourselves in the light of the goodness of God. When you look at things through the righteousness of God, your life becomes beautiful because you're looking at the world with new eyes from God's perspective instead of what man thinks. If a person understands the righteousness of God, it will take away wrath, anger, envy, malice, and every demeaning thing. The eyes of righteousness are the eyes of God. And when you look at people through the eyes of righteousness, everybody has value to you (including yourself).

Sometimes people think Christianity is about going to church, singing, listening to a preacher, giving your offering, then going back home. But Christianity is about exuding the righteousness, the goodness of God. Everything about you becomes a blessing. Everywhere you go, you impart the goodness of God. When you become conscious of the righteousness of God, you live a different kind of life. You live a life of completeness. You live from the mountaintop. You live a life without lack because His righteousness gives you everything you need. You never again have to wonder if God is pleased with you. That's the righteousness of God. You don't have to attain it. It has already been given to you. Many don't understand. They look at the righteousness of God from its results rather than from its source. But right living is not righteousness. It is a result of righteousness.

Many believe that if they can "live right" then they will have the righteousness of God. But that's not the case. You can never become righteous by living right. It's not possible. How can you live what you don't have? If I told you to go outside and park your Lamborghini and you don't have a Lamborghini, that would be impossible for you to do. You would not be able to do it because you just don't have what it takes to do what is being asked of you. In similar fashion, unless and until you are righteous, God does not expect you to live righteously. That would be unfair of God to ask you to do what is not possible for you to do. Therefore, He gives you righteousness first so that through the gift of that righteousness you can then live righteously. Once you receive the gift of righteousness, now you can live right and not the other way around.

Get Off the Righteousness Roller Coaster

That reminds me of another old song that says, "If you live right, Heaven belongs to you." Sleight of hand preachers and leaders love songs like this. I suspect this may even be their theme song! It is messages like this, whether spoken or sung, that leave people feeling like they can never be good enough. When they make mistakes, they feel like all is lost, and then when they feel like they are living right, they're on top of the world again. Can you see how such wrong thinking will create a roller coaster spiritual life?

It is the life of a baby Christian and it's about time that you stepped and walk in the light of who you really are. God does not want you to live a yo-yo life, one day up and another day down. He wants you to stay up, and the only way you can do that is to know that you have been given the righteousness of God. Watch what the Bible says in the book of Hebrews:

Hebrews 5:12-13
For when for the time ye ought to be teachers, ye have need that one teach you again which be the first principles of the oracles of God; and are become such as have need of milk, and not of strong meat. For every one that useth milk is unskilful in the word of righteousness: for he is a babe.

Paul calls those that are unskilful in the word of righteousness babes in Christ. The Greek word translated as unskilful in that passage is apeiros, and it literally means ignorant. So then, those that are ignorant of the word of righteousness are the nepios, the babes in Christ still needing deliverance fifteen years after receiving Christ. The root of the problem is the misconception of what righteousness is.

Imagine, a man like the apostle Paul on the road to Damascus going to kill Christians, caught red-handed by the Lord Jesus Christ himself, could lift up his hand and say I know nothing against me.

1 Corinthians 4:3-4
But with me it is a very small thing that I should be judged of you, or of man's judgment: yea, I judge not mine own self. For I know nothing by myself; yet am I not hereby justified: but He that judgeth me is the Lord.

Paul was actually telling them, my conscience is clear, I don't know anything against myself. Either Paul was suffering from some serious memory loss, or he knew something that his audience was not aware of. He was not confused about who he was. He was no longer sin conscious but righteousness conscious.

People are beaten up enough outside. They don't need to come into the house of God and be beaten again. Heaven does not belong to you because you live right. Heaven belongs to you because you have been made righteous, and it is that righteousness that will produce right living. This is righteousness, the nature of God. Preach it. Teach it. Help people to understand that God has made them righteous in Christ Jesus, and that it is a gift. You don't have to struggle for it, you don't have to attain it. It is a gift!

This is what Jesus came to do. He came to give you a new life. A life of righteousness. He came to make you a champion in life. He came to make you a success. And everything you require to fulfil all that God has called you to be has already been given to you. It is a righteous thing with God to do you good. It is His righteousness to be good to you because that it His nature. It is consistent with His righteousness to channel all necessary resources toward you so that you don't lack anything. This has to be your mentality. You have to accept this as your reality. You have everything that you require to fulfil all that God has called you to do.

Righteousness Is Not A Reward

The dictionary defines reward as something given in exchange for good behaviour or good work. When it comes to your righteousness before God, reward has nothing to do it. It's not about reward, rather it's about receiving. If righteousness was a reward for good works, we would all be in trouble! I came across a funny story recently that illustrates my point.

Three men died and went to Heaven. At the pearly gates, Jesus met them and said, "I will ask you each a question. If you tell the truth I will allow you into Heaven, but if you lie, Hell is waiting for you." Then the Lord asked the first man, "Did you ever cheat on your wife?" The first man answered and said, "Lord, I have never cheated on my wife." The Lord said, "Well done! For your reward, not only will I let you into Heaven, but you get the biggest mansion and a chauffeur driven Rolls Royce." Then the Lord asked the second man the same question, "Did you ever cheat on your wife?" The second man said, "Lord, I have to confess I'm afraid I did cheat on my wife twice." The Lord said, "I'll let you into Heaven. But for your unfaithfulness, you'll get a four-bedroom house and a Mercedes Benz." Then the Lord asked the third man the same question, "Did you ever cheat on your wife?" The third man hung his head and answered, "Lord, I'm ashamed to admit I cheated on my wife eight times." The Lord said, "True to My word, I'll still let you into Heaven. But for your unfaithfulness, you'll get a studio apartment and a VW Beetle." A little while later, the second and the third man saw the first man crying. They asked him, "Why are you crying? We thought you'd be happy with your big mansion and chauffeur driven Rolls Royce." The first man answered and said, "I was until I saw my wife ride by on a skateboard!"

Ladies and gentlemen, this is a funny story, but the truth is, if we based our righteousness on being rewarded for good works, though we might all make it to Heaven, we would all be scooting around on skateboards! God loves us independent of our performance. He isn't determining our righteousness based on our actions. Understanding this motivates us to serve God out of love instead of serving God out of fear that we're going to be punished, rejected, or that our prayers won't be answered. Settle it in your heart once and for all that you have the righteousness of Christ.

Chapter Three

Faith vs Grace

There are millions of people who struggle in their day-to-day walk as believers because they do not understand or know how to receive the wonderful gifts of faith and grace. Some have been improperly taught, and others have not been taught at all. I intend to correct that through this book. Another dynamic of the struggle is the "I can do it by myself!" attitude that causes some people to miss out on the blessings of what Christ has already done for them.

I need you to follow very closely as we go a bit deeper into this subject. During one of my semesters at university, I was a few days away from taking a final examination in a very difficult course. The course was required, only one professor taught it, and He wrote the book for the course. The result of this examination would determine whether each of us in the class passed the course or not. Prior to the examination, the professor gave us some instructions to prepare us. He told us that on the day of the examination he would hand out the papers with the exam questions on it, but we would not need to answer the questions. All we would need to do is to put our names on the exam sheet, turn it back in, and we would get an 'A' in the course. We listened in disbelief as he told us we would not even need to study for the examination. My classmates and I looked around at each other with raised eyebrows and puzzled expressions. This was an offer that seemed too good to be true. It just seemed as if there was a catch somewhere. Surely this couldn't be all we had to do to pass the most difficult course of the semester.

The professor went on to further explain that if we chose to answer the questions anyway, we would be graded on our own work instead of his original offer. He warned us that the test would be extremely difficult, and that only one person had ever been able to pass it. He reiterated that if we wanted to be sure we would pass the exam, all we would need to do is to come to the place where the exam would be given, put our names on the paper, and turn it back in. That's all. After the class, I could overhear some of the conversations of my classmates. Most of them thought the professor's offer was just too good to be true. Some thought there had to be some kind of trick behind it, and so they made up their minds to study even harder.

On the day of the examination, we filed into the classroom and silently took our seats. People were glancing around at each other wondering if what the professor had told us before was really true. The professor made his way down each aisle handing a copy of the examination paper to each student. As I received my paper, I reviewed the examination. The questions were extremely difficult! There was no way I would be able to write this exam and pass it! To make things worse, it was an essay exam. There were no multiple choice or true and false questions. There was no room for lucky guesses on this one!

For a moment, I panicked because even though I too thought the professor's offer was too good to be true, I had believed him and so I had not studied. But then, I reminded myself of the guarantee that he had given us: just put your name on the exam sheet, turn it in, and you'll pass the exam. As I looked around the room, most of my classmates were already furiously writing, racing against the clock to complete each answer on their exams. They chose to do their own work instead of accepting the professor's offer. I looked down at my sheet, looked up at the professor, and made my decision. I wrote my name on the sheet and nothing else.

Before I turned in my paper, I decided to sit for a while longer just to see what other people would do. Apparently, only a few believed the professor's generous offer and quickly handed in their papers with just their names on it. The others worked through the exam, agonizing over every answer. Then after carefully reviewing all their hard work, they handed in their papers. I watched as one by one they walked out of the classroom mentally exhausted and visibly defeated. Despite all their hard work, they still felt unsure as to whether they had done enough to earn an acceptable passing grade. They had not. They could not. They failed miserably! On the other hand, all of us who had accepted the professor's offer passed the course with flying colours. What an awesome exercise this was to show the wonderful grace of God!

This is an example of how many believers treat the righteousness of God. They find it difficult to believe that there is nothing that they need to do to earn a "passing grade" from Him. So they keep trying in their own efforts and failing miserably. What they fail to understand is that the very difficult test that was necessary to earn our righteousness had already been given to Jesus. He has already completed the course to the Father's satisfaction. The reality is, like my professor's examination, only one person was able to get all the answers right. And that person is not you or I, it is Jesus.

All the things you have been trying to do in order to please God are futile. There is only one thing you have to do and that is accept what Christ has done and that is enough to make you right with God. I want you to see something very interesting in scripture.

1 Corinthians 15:34
Awake to righteousness and sin not...

Now, right there I know we have a problem because many think if they tell the world that this is a sin and that is a sin it will solve the moral issues of the world. And even though you have heard it from the pulpit, I assure you that is not Bible. The scripture says awake to righteousness, and sin not. In other words, the only thing that will stop you from sinning is when you become righteousness conscious and not sin conscious. The opposite of what the verse says is also true, awake to sin consciousness and continue to sin. So, what the Bible bashers who are preaching the power of sin in church instead of the gift of God are actually doing is driving you to sin no matter how much you tell yourself that you are not going to do it. I know we have already dealt with righteousness but felt somebody needed to hear that. Now back to the exam.

The good news for us is because Jesus has already met all the requirements for passing that test, no one else was or is required to take the exam. That is the grace extended to us by the Father. You don't need to study for it, work for it, or be good enough for it. The only thing that you are required to do is to believe that the provisions for passing the examination have already been met by Jesus, and by faith "sign your name" to accept the offer. It's not about what you do, but what Christ has already done for you. It is a gift!

Ephesians 4:23-24
And be renewed in the spirit of your mind; and that ye put on the new man, which after God is created in righteousness and true holiness.

Brothers and sisters stop trying to be holy. You were born into it. The Bible says you were created in righteousness and true holiness. In other words, there is a false holiness out there that is being preached in our churches today, but the true holiness and righteousness is the one you received when you got born again. As simple as that sounds, the biggest challenge some people have with grace and faith is that they don't know how to simply receive them as gifts. They believe that even if they receive one, they have to work for the other, not realizing that both faith and grace are gifts from God.

I know, I said faith is a gift and now someone is wondering what about Romans 10:17. Let me break it down for you:

So then faith cometh by hearing, and hearing by the word of God.

Faith is a gift, but you will never be able to make use of something that you do not know that you have. Everything that we have inherited in Christ is in the Word of God, and the only way to know about it and use it is when you get into the Word. Let me ask you this one thing, who did Jesus die for? He died for the whole world. "For God so loved the world, that He gave His only begotten Son," not just for the Christians but for the whole world. So how come the whole world is not saved if God gave His Son for the world? Some have not heard about it, and they cannot receive what they don't know. This is why you can't just say I don't need the Word because I have received the gift of faith because it is the Word that tells you what that faith can do and that you have it. But let's look at what the book of Ephesians has to say on the matter.

Ephesians 2:8
For by grace are ye saved through faith; and that not of yourselves: it is the gift of God.

Paul is telling us that the salvation you have right now came by the grace of God through faith, and that faith is not of yourself but the gift of God. For you to even find it in your heart to believe in Christ and have faith to be born again, that faith you used was the gift of God that you could only receive and exercise after hearing the good news of God's grace. You don't have to work for either one. You need only to receive them and put them to work for you. It is really all about your receiving. But that is for a later chapter.

A gift that you have to work for is not a gift. There are some people who give gifts, but they have what we call "strings attached." This kind of giving is usually with an underlying motive to somehow manipulate or control the one who is receiving the gift. But God is not that way. Every gift He gives us is good. The Bible puts it this way:

James 1:17
Every good gift and every perfect gift is from above, and comes down from the Father of lights, with whom there is no variation or shadow of turning.

I love the way The Message translation puts the last part of the verse: "there is nothing deceitful in God, nothing two-faced, nothing fickle." That means if God gives you a gift, you can rest assured that it is good. It is for your highest and best benefit, and it is given with no strings attached.

Grace and faith are gifts from a good God who gives good gifts. Using our previous illustration, Jesus did all of the work and passed the exam, but we get the benefits of the 'A.' That's the good news of salvation! We put our faith (which is a gift from God) in Jesus and what He has already done, and we (by the gift of grace) get what He earned and deserves. It's not about what you do right, it's about what He has already done right. You can't find a better deal than that!

Many don't know this but, grace and faith must be balanced, and the pivot for that balance is righteousness. Righteousness, in simple terms, means to be in right standing or right relationship with God. This can only happen through total faith and dependence upon Christ and what He has already done. There is no other way.

Many believers fail to recognize how we become right in the sight of God. There are some who believe that God determines our righteousness based on what we do. That's not true. Yes, there is a relationship between our actions and our right standing with God, but it is right relationship with God that produces actions, not the other way around. That is to say, we are not made righteous by what we do. Righteousness is a gift that comes from God to those who accept what Jesus has done for them by faith. As it says in Romans 5:17-18 (CJB):

For if, because of the offence of one man, death ruled through that one man; how much more will those receiving the overflowing grace, that is, the gift of being considered righteous, rule in life through the one man Yeshua the Messiah! In other words, just as it was through one offence that all people came under condemnation, so also it is through one righteous act that all people come to be considered righteous.

Let me break it down for you this way. If our good works were weighed in the balances against God's righteousness, we would come up short every time. It would be like trying to balance a trillion bars of gold (God's righteousness) on one side of the scale with a feather (your works) on the other side. God's righteousness is always going to be more in quantity and quality than yours will ever be. In fact, this is why in Isaiah 64:6 it tells us that compared to God's righteousness, "all of our righteousness is like filthy rags." Jesus is the only one whose righteousness can balance the scales.

You see, Jesus was in right relationship with God as no one else could be. If being right with God was the exam, He was the only one who passed and everyone else failed. He is the Son of God. He is God manifest in the flesh. He is holy and pure and without sin, yet He became sin for us through no wrongdoing on His part.

2 Corinthians 5:21
Christ didn't have any sin. But God made him become sin for us.

So we can be made right with God because of what Christ has done for us.

In return for Jesus taking our sin, when we put our faith in Him we get His righteousness instead of our own. In other words, it's not our actions that make us acceptable to the Father. It's our trust in Jesus and what He has done that puts us in right standing with God.

Some of you are frustrated right now because you are trying to establish a right relationship with God through your own good works. That's like trying to unlock someone else's door with your own key. No matter how hard you try, it won't work! It is important for you to understand that this righteousness does not come from what you do. It comes from God as a gift. That's grace! And that grace is not based on whether you are reading the Bible enough, praying enough, going to church enough, tithing enough, or doing whatever enough! I know I just messed up somebody's theology right there. But this is what Paul meant in Romans when he told us:

Romans 11:6
But if it is by grace [God's unmerited favor], it is no longer on the basis of works, otherwise grace is no longer grace [it would not be a gift but a reward for works].

There are no two ways about it. You must trust completely in what Jesus did for you to obtain right relationship with God. Any trust in your own goodness will shift you away from grace. In fact, this is exactly what millions of people in the body of Christ are doing today. They receive salvation by putting total faith in Christ for the forgiveness of their sins, but then they live like God still relates to them on the basis of their works, even after their salvation.

This was Paul's biggest source of frustration with the Galatians. He would be pulling his hair out if he could see the state of the Church today! Watch what the scripture says:

Galatians 2:21
I do not frustrate the grace of God, for if righteousness come by the law, then Christ is dead in vain.

Paul is telling them, by trying to earn your own righteousness you are denying the very sacrifice of Christ, because if you can do it by yourself, then Christ died for nothing.

So, if you are a believer and you find yourself feeling guilty or condemned, it's a sure sign that you have failed to understand this truth. Satan's only inroad into our lives is sin. But, if we understand our right standing with God on the basis of what Jesus did for us, and not by our own actions, then Satan's power to condemn is gone. Those who live with a feeling of unworthiness are not trusting in God's righteousness but are looking to their own actions to obtain right standing with God. They have not properly understood the balance of grace and faith and their relationship to each other. They'll be left feeling exhausted and defeated like the students in the class who chose to do their own work rather than receive the offer of grace.

By definition, the word grace means unmerited, unearned, undeserved favour. Therefore, the good news is grace has nothing to do with what you do. Grace existed before you ever came to be. Another way of saying it is, grace is God's part. Faith, on the other hand, is defined as being a positive response to what God has already provided by grace. Faith only makes use of what God has already provided for you. Therefore, faith is your part.

Ephesians 2:8-9
For by grace are ye saved through faith; and that not of yourselves: it is the gift of God: Not of works, lest any man should boast.

I don't want you to miss this because a profound truth is being declared here in this verse. It says we are saved by grace through faith, not one or the other. Think of it this way—grace is what God does; faith is what you do. Your part is simple: respond to His grace by faith and make use of what has already been accomplished. For instance, if you think of the earlier illustration, grace is the offer to take the examination with no work on your part. Faith is signing your name to the paper to accept the offer. Faith makes use of what God has already provided. This is how grace and faith work together.

Andrew Wommack, a well-known Bible teacher puts it this way: "Many emphasize grace and others emphasize faith. But too few emphasize balancing grace and faith. It's like sodium and chloride: Taken individually, both are poisons and can kill you. When mixed together, they become salt, which you must have to live. Grace without your positive response of faith won't save you, and faith that isn't a response to God's grace will bring you into condemnation. But, put your faith in what God has already done for you, and you have the victory that overcomes the world (1 John 5:4)."

God has done His part by giving His Son, Jesus. His grace has provided everything through the sacrifice of Jesus. There is absolutely nothing you can do to earn it and nothing you can do to lose it. God's grace has provided not only for salvation but also for every need of your life. He anticipated every need you could ever have and has met those needs through Jesus even before you existed. It's already a done deal!

Have you fallen into the trap of thinking God's response is linked to your performance? Are you tired of feeling unworthy? Are you ready to live a life free of guilt and condemnation? Simply remember to put your faith in what God has already done, not in what you do. This is how you balance grace with faith.

Chapter Four

No More Sin Consciousness

How can you tell if you are really walking in grace or trusting in the grace of God or not? One of the distinguishing characteristics about grace is that when you are relating to God on the basis of what He's done instead of what you've done, everything God has done is already past tense. It's already a finished work. It's accomplished. When you start feeling like you've got to obtain this, and you've got to work to do that, when it becomes work and struggle instead of rest, you've moved out of God's grace.

God's grace is a position of rest and peace. Watch what the scripture says in 1 Peter 5:7:

Casting the whole of your care [all your anxieties, all your worries, all your concerns, once and for all] on Him, for He cares for you affectionately and cares about you watchfully.

What most believers do not realise is that fear and anxiety work against you, and it is one of the major inroads that the enemy uses to oppress the people of God. Imagine, the Bible says 'fear not' 366 times. You have a 'fear not' for every day of the year. There is a good reason for that. The born again Christian is at his peak strength when he is full of joy and peace.

This is why when you watch most people during the Sunday service they feel like they can run through a wall. Because of the word they are receiving, they're full of joy and faith, and at that moment all things are possible. But by the time they get to Wednesday and start thinking about how they are going to cope because the rent is due on Friday, immediately depression sets in, fear and dread become the norm, and this is exactly where the enemy would like to keep you, without any hope.

But when you look unto Jesus, the Author and the Finisher of our faith, all things are possible. Suddenly, you realise that His grace is sufficient for you. This is when you can dance in the rain, boldly declare, "I can do all things through Christ which strengthens me!" I'm telling you, at this level, your circumstances will have no choice but to line up with what you choose to focus on. You will no longer be "under the circumstances." Hallelujah! That is how you take advantage of grace.

So, if you're taking care [anxious or worried or concerned] about things, if the weight of things is getting on you, you are not moving in God's grace. You've moved back into performance mode. You're trying to earn it. Anxiety, worry, and concern are all rooted in fear, and the only fear that you can have is when you are operating in the flesh (allowing the flesh to control you). But this kind of joy I'm talking about doesn't just come because your landlord has changed his mind about collecting the rent that month. No. It is a result of the assurance and certainty of what Christ has done and how He has given you victory over the prevailing situation.

Acts 16:25-26
But at midnight Paul and Silas were praying and singing hymns to God, and the prisoners were listening to them. Suddenly there was a great earthquake, so that the foundations of the prison were shaken; and immediately all the doors were opened and everyone's chains were loosed.

This is why Paul and Silas could sing praises to God in what seemed to be their darkest hour. In the midst of it all, there was a joy that was welling up on the inside of them to the extent that the chains that were binding them had no choice but to fall off. I can assure you that would have never happened if they had sat in that jail cell complaining about how unfair life is with the other inmates.

When you are in worry or fear, it's because you aren't trusting in God and Paul and Silas knew better than to allow even the fear of death to move their focus from the grace of God. There is no fear when you trust in God. Look at what 1 John 4:18 says:

There is no fear in love; but perfect love casteth out fear: because fear hath torment. He that feareth is not made perfect in love.

Remember God Himself is love, and when you choose to focus on who He is and what He has done there is no room for fear. If you walk in God's perfect love, you won't walk in fear. That does not mean that fear won't come, but it will not dominate you or control your thoughts and behaviour. Fear comes like a bird of prey to attack your mind. But like the saying goes, you can't stop a bird from flying over your head, but you can keep it from making a nest there. It's up to you to choose whether or not you walk in fear or live daily in the love and grace of God.

It's in There

When you received Christ, He came with everything you need to live this life victoriously. If the only purpose for salvation was to take you to Heaven, then we would have a firing squad waiting for you after answering the altar call so they could check you straight into the pearly gates. Let me use this illustration to make my point. In 1982, the Campbell Soup Company introduced an advertising campaign for a brand of pasta sauce called Prego. The drive and focus of the campaign were to make the point that nothing needed to be added to the sauce because "It's in there." This was the slogan for Prego, and this is the slogan for grace.

This is exactly why when Peter saw Aeneas, a brother in the Lord who had been bedridden for eight years, was paralysed and could not walk, his response was simply amazing. Watch what the scripture says:

Acts 9:33-34
And there he found a certain man named Aeneas, which had kept his bed eight years, and was sick of the palsy. And Peter said unto him, Aeneas, Jesus Christ maketh thee whole: arise, and make thy bed. And he arose immediately.

All that Peter is saying there is that the Jesus you are carrying whom you have believed when He comes into your life, the healing that you need right now He brought with Him. It comes with it! Now don't get me wrong, as anointed as Peter was he did not bring the healing. Aeneas was sitting on that healing for eight years until he heard those words coming out of the mouth of Peter. All he needed to do was to awaken to the reality of the grace that God had already provided for his healing.

When you are thinking of God's grace, everything you'll ever need and everything God has called you to do in your life is already accomplished in God. "It's in there!" The anointing that it takes to produce it is already there. You don't have to do something to get God to anoint you. In fact, there are two types of prayers that God actually cannot hear. First of all, when you pray asking God to do something He has already done and secondly when you ask Him to do something that He sent you to do.

1 John 5:14
Now this is the confidence that we have in Him, that if we ask anything according to His will, He hears us.

The Bible says, when we ask according to His will He hears us. So, no matter how much you shout when you pray, as long as what you're asking for falls into those two categories, He can't even hear you.

This is why you cannot be praying to God asking to be anointed. You are already anointed! If you are striving to get God's anointing you aren't walking in grace. It would be unjust for God to call you to do a supernatural ministry and expect you to do it without His power and anointing.

1 John 2:20
But you have an unction from the Holy One, and ye know all things.

God would not call you to do something without giving you the power to fulfil it. So, if you are called, you are also anointed. It's already there. It's a matter of resting in it rather than working to get it. When you walk in faith in what God's already done, then you have peace. The apostle Paul is a perfect example of how to operate in the grace that God has given. Paul is a man that was used by God to write nearly two-thirds of the New Testament, and if anyone knew how to take advantage of the grace of God, it was this guy. Let's go back to scripture:

1 Corinthians 15:10
But by the grace of God I am what I am: and His grace which was bestowed upon me was not in vain; but I laboured more abundantly than they all: yet not I, but the grace of God which was with me.

Are you getting this? Paul attributes his success to one thing, the grace of God. At first, he says I worked but actually, it was God's grace doing it. In other words, when the grace of God is working, you don't need to do anything, just like Paul. But notice he says, His grace which was bestowed upon me was not in vain. That means you can have the same grace and it be in vain. How? When you become conscious of your own works and forget what God has done. When we are out of peace and trying to work and perform and make something happen, that's evidence that we are not walking in the grace of God. What you need is the full assurance of the understanding of grace.

Full Assurance

Paul the Apostle recognized this area of need in the Church and expresses his desire for the fulfilment of it. In **Colossians 2:2 (KJV) he says:**

That their hearts might be comforted, being knit together in love, and unto all riches of the full assurance of understanding, to the acknowledgement of the mystery of God, and of the Father, and of Christ;

Paul's desire and prayer was that you would have the full assurance of understanding. That suggests that there are different levels of seeing and understanding these truths. He wants you to receive all of the riches of the full assurance of understanding, and to acknowledge—accept and admit the truth of—God's mystery. And what is that mystery? It is Christ in you, the hope of glory.

Colossians 1:27
To them God would make known what are the riches of the glory of this mystery among the Gentiles, which is Christ in you, the hope of glory.

He wants you to acknowledge that Christ is already here. You are no longer trying to get to God. He's already here. He is in you. If you could see and understand that God is already in you, how could you wonder whether you're going to make it if God himself is already in you? That can only happen when you don't really have a revelation of that. There are many believers who live and act as though they are trying to get God in them. Or they think if they mess up, God leaves and they have to try to get Him back by proving how good they are. God is not some kind of divine yo-yo that is tied to you by the string of your good works. He's not a here today, gone tomorrow God. He's not a shifting and changing God. He's a stay put God and everything that He is and has stays with Him in you.

If you could only learn to rest in that assurance of truth and acknowledge and rely on the fact that God has already done what needs to be done, there would be so much power and peace in your life. Did you know that when you understand your right standing with God you'll get to the place where you can be quiet? Nothing moves you. Not even the devil himself.

Smith Wigglesworth, one of the great heroes of faith, told the story of an encounter with the devil. Mr. Wigglesworth was awakened from a deep sleep to the presence of the devil standing next to his bed. Wigglesworth looked at the devil, the devil looked at him, and then Smith said with a sigh, "Oh, it's just you." And with that, he rolled over and went back to sleep.

That's the kind of peace, quietness, and confidence a person who understands the assurance of his or her right standing with God can have! When you rest in the reality of what Christ has already accomplished, you can face every day and every challenge with the confident affirmation, I am who God says I am, I can do what He says I can do. I have what He says I have.

You Complete Me

Now, there is a line from a popular 90's movie that says, "I love you. You complete me." If God had written the script, the line

Grace Driven Life

would be "I love you. I have completed you!" There is a completeness that you need to be conscious of because you are in Christ.

Colossians 2:9-10
For in Him dwelleth all the fulness of the Godhead bodily. And ye are complete in Him, which is the head of all principality and power.

Notice it does not say you are going to be complete in Christ. You are already complete in Him. According to John 1:14, Jesus is full of grace and truth. That's a glorious truth! And here's where it gets even better for us. Watch what the scripture says:

Colossians 2:16
And of His fulness have all we received, and grace for grace.

You have received His fulness! You didn't get a little dab of God. You got every bit of God that God could give you and it's all right there in your spirit. You're already complete in Him. There's nothing more to get! You can't get more anointing. You can't get more faith. You can't get more righteous. You can't get more holy. You can't get more pleasing to God. It's all already there. Now, you can renew your mind to it and receive more anointing manifest, receive more faith in operation in your life, you can walk in more joy; but the truth is, you've already got it all. If we really believed and understood this simple truth, it would do away with discouragement, fear, and everything that causes us to feel that we are not everything God wants us to be.

What Sin?

Now I want to look at something that most believers struggle with almost on the daily. God never withdraws anything that He's given to us. What happens is sometimes when certain things happen, your conscience tells you that you are not worthy of the blessings He has given. As a result, you feel that God is no longer close to you or you are no longer close to Him. But, the reality is you can't get any closer to God than you already are because He is inside of you. All you need to do is acknowledge that reality. Don't wait for a feeling. Know and acknowledge that He is right there.

The book of Hebrews is a powerful book on the subject of grace. In chapter 8:10-12, it says:

For this is the covenant that I will make with the house of Israel after those days, saith the Lord; I will put my laws into their mind, and write them in their hearts: and I will be to them a God, and they shall be to me a people: And they shall not teach every man his neighbour, and every man his brother, saying, Know the Lord: for all shall know me, from the least to the greatest. For I will be merciful to their unrighteousness, and their sins and their iniquities will I remember no more.

You are righteous. That is an established reality. But God knows that there may be times when you might not act like who you are. Therefore, He has promised you that He will be merciful to you even if you act in an unrighteous manner. So, if you mess up and Satan the accuser tries to make you feel condemned, you need only remind yourself of this covenant promise that God says, "I will be merciful to their unrighteousness." Not only that, but God went further to say, "their sins and their iniquities will I remember no more."

God is assuring you of the completeness of His forgiveness. Not only will He be merciful to you if you mess up, but He chooses in advance to not even remember any wrongdoing. Before you get a chance to remember it, He has already forgotten it. Now, do you think if God chooses not to remember any wrongdoing that you might have done that He wants you to walk around constantly reminding yourself of it and beating yourself up over it? Absolutely not! There's a beautiful verse that assures us of this in 1 John 3:20 (TPT) which says:

Whenever our hearts make us feel guilty and remind us of our failures, we know that God is much greater and more merciful than our conscience, and he knows everything there is to know about us.

God never wants you to walk around with a guilty conscience. Instead, He wants you to be conscious of His love, mercy, and grace toward you in every situation.

You see, we have something far superior to what those living under the Old Covenant had. We have what Hebrews refers to time and again as a "better covenant." Under the Old Covenant, there was a system established whereby sacrifices had to be made year after year in order for the people to be right with God. But there were two major problems with this system. First of all, the sacrifice was never enough to remove sin, only to cover it for a short while. Secondly, as soon as sacrifices were made, the people would go out and sin again creating the need for yet another sacrifice to be offered. That imperfect system was just a shadow of better things to come.

Hebrews 10:1-4

For the law, having a shadow of the good things to come, and not the very image of the things, can never with these same sacrifices, which they offer continually year by year, make those who approach perfect. For then would they not have ceased to be offered? For the worshipers, once purified, would have had no more consciousness of sins. But in those sacrifices there is a reminder of sins every year. For it is not possible that the blood of bulls and goats could take away sins.

An imperfect sacrifice could not perfect or purify the people so that they would no longer have any guilt or consciousness of sin. That is understood by the verse. But, the verse is also implicitly saying that if there was a sacrifice that could make us perfect, then we would be purified and have no more consciousness of sins. That is what Christ did as the perfect sacrifice. He perfected and purified us so that we no longer have guilt or consciousness of sins. As Hebrews 10:10 succinctly puts it, "we have been sanctified through the offering of the body of Jesus Christ once and for all." Now, that's something to shout about!

The Wrong Confessional

One of the biggest misconceptions in the Church today is that even though you are forgiven at the point of salvation, if you ever mess up there is hell to pay. Most Christians believe that once they become born again their slates are wiped clean, and they have a brand new start. At the same time, they also believe that if they mess up it's going to be held against them. This is why in a lot of churches, when an altar call is made for people to come and get "right with God," born again believers are among the first to bum-rush the altar. Why does this happen? It happens because they've developed a sin consciousness again.

Let me tell you something, the Lord Jesus didn't shed His blood just to give us a "clean until you mess up" slate. The Bibles says He obtained for us "eternal redemption."

Hebrews 9:11-12
But Christ being come an high priest of good things to come, by a greater and more perfect tabernacle, not made with hands, that is to say, not of this building; Neither by the blood of goats and calves, but by His own blood he entered once into the Holy place, having obtained eternal redemption for us.

If you really understand eternal redemption, you understand that sin is no longer and will never be a problem between you and God. You may be wondering how this can be so. Let me explain.

Jesus shed His blood and died for the forgiveness of sin over 2000 years ago. According to the scriptures, He died for the sins of the world, that means everyone in it and everyone that would be in it. For the sake of our discussion, let's narrow down "the world" to just you and me. Now, when He died on the cross He died for your sins and mine. But neither of us were there, right? We weren't even born yet. Which means, He died for sins that you and I had not even committed yet. Since we were not born, any sin we could commit was in the future. Are you with me so far?

That means that the Blood of Jesus covered not only the sins of the people who were alive before Jesus, and the sins of the people who were alive at the time He died on the cross, but also the sins that were yet to be committed. So, Jesus died for sins past, present, and future. Think about it. If He didn't pay for your sins in advance of you committing them, then you could not have gotten born again. Your sins have already been dealt with... all of them!

From childhood I have heard preachers teach that believers need to confess their sins to the Lord in order to keep their right standing and peace with God. The scripture they love to quote is in 1 John. Watch what the Bible says:

1 John 1:9
If we confess our sins, He is faithful and just to forgive us our sins and to cleanse us from all unrighteousness.

I mean, this verse has been used to write books on confession, yet the messages of those books could not be further from the truth of what the Bible was actually teaching here. You need to remember that the author of that verse is the very same man who tells us in the fifth chapter of the same book that believers cannot sin.

1 John 5:18
We know that whosoever is born of God sinneth not, but he that is begotten of God keepeth himself, and that wicked one toucheth him not.

It's either John was missing something here, or we have got this whole thing twisted. But before we get deeper into that one, I want us to re-examine that verse in 1 John 1:9.

If we confess our sins, He is faithful and just to forgive us our sins and to cleanse us from all unrighteousness.

Many have been schooled in how they need to go through the ritual of reciting all their sins before they can be assured of forgiveness from God. Yet this is not what John was instructing us to do here. When the Bible talks about the confession of sins, it is not talking about you bringing God into remembrance of all the sins you have committed. Far from it!

That Greek word translated as confession in that passage is homologeo and the literal translation to the English is the word assent which means the expression of approval or agreement. So, with that understanding when you look at that verse you actually find that what John was saying is that, if you homologeo—come into agreement with what God says and has done about your sins—He is faithful and just to forgive us our sins and to cleanse us from all unrighteousness.

Your confession should be of what God says about your sins, how He has forgiven them, how they were nailed to the cross of Christ, how they were laid on Jesus, and no charge can be brought against you now. Hallelujah! Now notice what the previous verse says so that we don't miss the context of what is being said here:

1 John 1:8
If we say that we have no sin, we deceive ourselves, and the truth is not in us.

Now John is dealing with one thing here, that is what you say about sin, and he starts off by telling you that if you say that you have no sin, you are deceiving yourself. In other words, you cannot go around saying, I am not like so and so, I don't curse, I don't steal, I'm a pretty decent person. When you do that, you are actually saying that you can be righteous all by yourself and you do not need the sacrifice of Christ. And now that he has just told you what not to say about sin, he goes on to tell you what you ought to be saying about it in the very next verse. You can actually read the two in one breath. I don't how the Church has missed this.

If we confess—homologeo—our sins, He is faithful and just to forgive us our sins and to cleanse us from all unrighteousness.

That is what you ought to be saying about sin: the same thing that God says about it, that you are free from the curse of sin, it is no longer master over your life for whom the Son sets free is free indeed. Remember this is exactly how you got born again, simply by believing in your heart and saying the same thing about your salvation that God says.

Romans 10:9
That if thou shalt confess (homologeo) with thy mouth the Lord Jesus, and shalt believe in thine heart that God hath raised him from the dead, thou shalt be saved.

That same Greek word used in 1 John is the same word that Paul uses in the book of Romans. You homologeo (confess) the Lordship of Christ and how God raised Him from the dead and salvation is yours. Why on earth would you then assume that when John says, confess (homologeo) your sins he is talking about you making a list of your wrongs?

Do you know why even though the scripture says that, For God so loved the world that He gave His only begotten Son that whosoever believeth in Him should not perish, we still have people that have not received Christ? First of all, they have not believed, and they have not confessed (homologeo) what God has done for them. Yet Christ did for them and paid the same price that He did for you.

Can you imagine the peace and joy you rob yourself of by just failing to homologeo, confess, say what God has done and said about your sin? He has already paid the price, but believers today still carry the weight of sin that Christ paid for. It's tragic!

Perfectly Perfected

Brothers and sisters, God is not holding anything against you. It is important for you to get that. Hebrews 10:10 tells us that "we have been sanctified through the offering of the body of Jesus Christ once for all." Jesus did not shed His blood, die, and get up from the grave only to hand you a "cleansed from sin" coupon that has an expiration date on it. What Jesus did, the one-time sacrifice He made, was enough for all time. **Hebrews 10:11-14** says it this way:

And every priest stands ministering daily and offering repeatedly the same sacrifices, which can never take away sins. But this Man, after He had offered one sacrifice for sins forever, sat down at the right hand of God, from that time waiting till His enemies are made His footstool. For by one offering He has perfected forever those who are being sanctified.

Did you catch the last part of verse 13? You are perfected. It's not your flesh that's perfected. Your body isn't what was made new when you got saved. If you were fat or skinny, short or tall before you got saved, you'll be fat or skinny, short or tall after you get saved (unless, of course, a miracle has occurred in your body). The point is, your flesh didn't get born again. And your emotional side, the soulish part of you, didn't get born again. Your spirit is what got born again, and that spirit was sanctified and perfected forever! It does not have to be wiped and cleansed from any defilement that you get living in this body. You are sealed with the Holy Ghost and there is nothing that can contaminate your spirit. The Blood of Jesus Christ cleansed you to such a degree that sin is not and never will be an issue between you and God.

Remember, God is Spirit and He relates to you on a spiritual level. So, if your spirit (which has been sealed by the Holy Ghost) is never contaminated, that means you can come before God with no consciousness of sin because there is no sin in your spirit. There's a part of you that's as pure as Jesus is pure because it is literally the Spirit of Jesus that is sent into your heart. According to 1 Corinthians 6:17, your spirit is joined with the Lord. Your spirit and the Spirit of Jesus are identical in holiness, power, love; they're identical in everything! Your spirit is perfect. Your spirit is pure. And God wants you to walk in the spirit and not in the flesh. He wants you to walk in what He has done for you instead of walking in what you think you can do for Him and wondering if it is enough. In the Spirit everything is complete. You're not trying to be holy. You are already holy in God's sight.

Religious sleight of hand preachers and teacher always deal with the outer man—the body and the soul. Like the Pharisees, they always want you to focus on your actions and your feelings. God is not that way. He is not focused on the outward. He is always looking at and dealing with that hidden man of the heart which is your spirit. That's what God meant in 1 Samuel 16:7 when He told Samuel that man always looks on the outward appearance, but He is always looking at the heart. God has not changed. He still looks at the inner man, your spirit.

Grace Is Waiting

Your spirit is the main part of you. However, that does not mean that you should neglect your body or your soul. We are spirit, soul, and body and we live in all three realms. But when it comes to relating to God, you can only approach Him in spirit and in truth. God does not love the Church based on action. He loves the Church based on the fact that we have put our faith in His Son as our Saviour. That being said, our actions should parallel our spirit. God wants the Church to act like the righteous love-filled people we are because this is how all men will know that we are His disciples. He wants our righteousness to be worked out so that it manifests in our bodies and lifestyle. So, in that sense, we do need to maintain righteousness, but not so that we can be right with God. Remember, our actions do not make us righteous, but our righteousness—once we understand, receive, and operate in the consciousness of it—will produce right actions.

It is important to note that while God relates to you based on your spirit which is pure and holy and righteous, He does deal with your flesh. Let me be clear, God always fellowships with you based on who you are in the Spirit. Your born again spirit is off limits to the devil. As Stanley Kirk Burrell aka MC Hammer put it, you can't touch this! But, your flesh, if mishandled, is Satan's inroad into your life. For that reason, God will deal with you if you are mistreating your body, not for the purpose of rejecting you, but because He loves you and He does not want the enemy taking advantage of you. So, He will convict you if you start getting into sin or yielding to temptation. But also let's be clear on this point: if you get into sin and stop experiencing the love, peace, and joy and other blessings that you have been given, it is not because God withdrew those things from you. God's grace toward you never changes. If you stop experiencing those blessings, it's because you shifted away from the life of grace.

One of my favourite stories in the Bible is that of the Prodigal Son in Luke 15:11-22. In this account, there is a father who has two sons. The younger son decided he wanted to leave his father's house and go out there and sow his wild oats, as they say. So, he went to his father, asked for his inheritance, and got as far away from his father as he could. The Bible said he went to a faraway country. While he was there, he used up all his inheritance money in what some translations describe as reckless and immoral living (and that's putting it nicely). All the so-called friends he had made while he had money left him when he was broke. He ended up homeless, hungry, and hopeless. Then one day, he came to his senses and remembered what it used to be like living in his father's house. It was a blessed life! He said to himself, I'll go back to my father and tell him, "Dad, I messed up big time! I sinned against heaven and against you. I'm not good enough to be called your son anymore. Just treat me like one of your hired workers." And that's exactly what he did. He got up from where he was and headed back home.

Now, here's the part of the story I really like. The father had been waiting for him to come back. Every day, he would look out for his son coming back. On that particular day, he was looking out and saw his son approaching from a long way off. As soon as the father spotted his son, he ran the distance out to meet him, threw his arms around him, and covered his face with kisses. The son said, "Dad, I messed up big time! I sinned against heaven and against you. I'm not good enough to be called your son anymore." Before the son could get another word out, the father called for a big celebration in honour of the return of his son. This is the part I don't want you to miss. The father never even so much as acknowledged the wrongdoings of the son. All he cared about was that his son was back home and was now able to once again enjoy all of the benefits and blessings that rightfully belonged to him as a son. The father never changed in his love for his son, and the blessings that he had given to his son were still just as available to him as they always had been.

Why did I share that story with you? Perhaps you have shifted away from grace and have found yourself getting into a sinful lifestyle. Grace is waiting for you. Your blessings are still your blessings. Your relationship with your heavenly Father is still intact. He does not want you to be focused on your sins. He wants you to focus on His love and grace. You see, the son in the story thought he had lost everything, but really, he had lost nothing. All of his blessings were right where he left them. All he needed was to come to his senses and become conscious of that reality. The same is true of you. The sooner you realize that God's love for you has not and will never change, the sooner you reclaim all the blessings that are rightfully yours, the sooner you can start enjoying the life of grace again. The Father is waiting for you, not with punishment or rejection, but with outstretched arms, a loving embrace, and all the grace you could ever imagine. Your life is about to make a 360-degree turn. Now, stay with me. I'm about to turn up the heat in this next chapter.

Chapter Five

Grace as A Person

Do you remember when the children of Israel were in bondage in Egypt? For at least 400 years they were enslaved and subjected daily to harsh and oppressive conditions. In their distress, they cried out for a deliverer. In Exodus Chapter 3, the Bible says, that God saw the suffering and heard the cries of His people. And then God makes a very interesting statement. He says, "I am come down to deliver my people." God came down to bring salvation to His people. But how did He do it? He did it through a man named Moses. When God wants to bring salvation to His people, He sends a person. This is a biblical principle. Time and time again throughout the scriptures, God's people needed deliverance, and each time God would send a deliverer in the form of a person.

Now, in eternity past, God saw the world in bondage and knew that we needed salvation. But this time, He wanted our salvation to be permanent. So, before the foundation of the world, He planned to save us. And what did he do? He did what He did for the children of Israel. He came down to deliver us. How did He do it? He sent the Person of His Son, Jesus.

2 Corinthians 5:19
To wit, that God was in Christ, reconciling the world unto himself, not imputing their trespasses unto them; and hath committed unto us the word of reconciliation.

God already had a way out for us before we ever got into trouble. That's why the scripture says that Christ was crucified before the foundations of the earth. Remember, the God we serve establishes the end from the beginning. He already had an expected end for you. The plan of God was that the world would be saved through the gift of His Son, Jesus.

In 1 Corinthians 4:7, Paul asks a question: "What do you have that was not given to you?" Everything good that you have and everything that you'll ever need to live your best life has been given to you. And everything that God has given to you, including salvation, is by grace, and that grace is in Jesus Christ.

Ephesians 2:8
For by grace you have been saved through faith, and that not of yourselves; it is the gift of God

Salvation came to you in the person of Jesus Christ. The grace needed for salvation can only be found in Jesus Christ. It is of paramount importance for you to understand that this salvation is not only deliverance from bondage. It is that, but it so much more than that. In salvation is deliverance out of danger into safety; it means to be rescued from the power and penalty of sin; salvation brings love, healing, preservation, prosperity, and every blessing imaginable. Salvation is the grace of God made accessible to man, and that grace is packaged in the Person of Jesus Christ. He is the source of grace. That is why when you get Jesus, you get everything that grace has to offer.

John 10:10
The thief cometh not, but for to steal, and to kill, and to destroy: I am come that they might have life, and that they might have it more abundantly.

Contrary to common belief, the Greek word translated as life in that passage is not just talking about going to Heaven, but it is life as God has it, zoe. It's the God-kind of life where there is nothing missing and nothing broken. When God gave Christ, He gave His all for you.

Making Contact with Grace

Before we go further, I want to ask you a question. Is water wet? It seems a relatively simple question, doesn't it? But for some people it is a controversial topic. Most people would immediately agree that water is wet. However, there are scientists who would emphatically say that water is not wet. Their general premise, which is the school of thought I also follow, is that dampness is what happens when we experience or come into contact with water, but water itself is not wet. You may be wondering, what does the wetness of water have to do with Jesus and grace. Well, when it comes to the subject of Jesus and grace, that too for some is a controversial subject. Some say Jesus is grace. Here is what we believe. Jesus is not grace, but grace is what happens when we experience or come into contact with Jesus.

Grace is not the fourth member of the Trinity. Grace is a spiritual substance which can be imparted or given. This is why Paul would sometimes include the phrase, "Grace be unto you" when he was addressing the Church in his epistles. It is important to note that while Jesus is not grace, He is the very embodiment of grace.

John 1:14
And the Word became flesh and dwelt among us, and we beheld His glory, the glory as of the only begotten of the Father, full of grace and truth.

You see, Jesus is full of grace. There is as much grace in Jesus as is possible for Him to have, and outside of Him there is no grace to be had. This may be one of the reasons why some equate Jesus with grace. They are not one and same, yet they are inseparable. We are not saying if you've seen grace you've seen Jesus. We are saying that wherever you see Jesus, you see grace. The message of Christ is, in fact, the message of grace. Grace exposes the heart of Jesus. While He is not grace, you cannot have or experience grace without Him. This is a greater truth.

The Greater Truth About Grace

I know what I am teaching right now may sound alien to someone, yet you have been in the Church for a long time. The fact is, in the Bible, there are greater truths and there are lesser truths. It is a design strategy of God which we can see from the very beginning. For example, in Genesis 1:16 it says:

Then God made two great lights: the greater light to rule the day, and the lesser light to rule the night...

There is a greater light which is the sun, and a lesser light which is the moon. Did you know that the moon actually does not emit light on its own? It actually only reflects the light from the sun. That's pretty amazing considering how brightly we see the moon shining at night. It's even more amazing when you consider that even at its brightest, the moon is only reflecting at most 12% of the sun's light at any given time.

Jesus declared himself to be the Light of the world (John 8:12). At the same time, He says that you are the light of the world (Matthew 5:14). How can Jesus be the Light of the world and we be the light of the world at the same time? That's not a difficult question to answer when you understand greater truths and lesser truths. The greater truth is that Jesus is the Light. You, like the moon, do not produce your own light, yet you are also light. Your light comes from His Light. The lesser truth is contained in or a part of the greater truth. There is a greater truth and a lesser truth when it comes to grace. You do not produce your own grace. Your grace comes from His grace.

Throughout the scriptures, particularly the books written by Paul the Apostle, you will see the phrase, "the grace of our Lord Jesus Christ." When you see the word of, according to most dictionary definitions, it has to do with a measure or relationship between a part and a whole. What follows "of" is the whole, and what precedes it, is the part. So, when we read or say, "the grace of our Lord Jesus Christ," it means that Jesus is the whole and grace is a part of the whole. The lesser, grace, is contained in the greater, Jesus Christ.

God's Navigational System

When God wanted to give His grace to you, He didn't send a theological concept or a belief, He sent His Son. God knew you needed grace, so He designed a system whereby that need could be fulfilled. Let's look again at **Ephesians 2:8 (AMP):**

For it is by grace [God's remarkable compassion and favour drawing you to Christ] that you have been saved [actually delivered from judgment and given eternal life] through faith. And this [salvation] is not of yourselves [not through your own effort], but it is the [undeserved, gracious] gift of God;

Within this verse, is God's navigational system that brings grace to you. The way a TomTom or other GPS navigational system works is that you put in the address or location of where you want to go, and the system maps it out for you and gives you step by step directions to get there. Are you with me? Now, grace is the location that God knew you needed to get to, but He knew you would never find it on your own. So, He provided His own navigational system. His navigational system does not work like the ones we use on our smart devices or in our cars. His is so much better. As I said, with our GPS systems, we have to find the location. But with God's navigational system, the location finds us.

A lot of people when referring to their salvation say that they found God. But that's not how God's navigational system works. You don't find God for salvation, He finds you. Jesus said that He came to seek and to save that which was lost. You didn't find grace, grace found you, and that grace is located in Jesus. When you plug grace into your spiritual GPS, the only address you'll find is Jesus. He is the location and destination of grace. And, guess what? You're already there! Watch what Paul had to say about his own salvation:

Galatians 1:16
But when it pleased God, who separated me from my mother's womb, and called me by His grace, to reveal His Son in me, that I might preach Him among the heathen;

This is why the Bible calls us God's elect. You were handpicked by God, called by name, hallelujah! And we got there by the GPS of Jehovah for the Lord Jesus said, no man cometh to the Father except through Me. Are you getting this?

Let's look again at **John 1:14:**

And the Word became flesh and dwelt among us, and we beheld His glory, the glory as of the only begotten of the Father, full of grace and truth.

Jesus is the Word become flesh. He is full of grace meaning He is the source of grace and the embodiment of grace. He is the personification of grace. That is to say, He is the perfect example of grace. The fullness of the grace of Jesus Christ is yours. You cannot get more grace, but you can grow in grace. Growing in grace is what makes the difference between a life of reigning and a life of straining. The question is, how do you grow in grace? The answer to that question is one you cannot afford to miss. Stay with me, we are just getting warmed up. I want to show in the next chapter how you can grow in grace. So, keep reading, and you will soon find out.

Chapter Six

Growing in Grace

In my personal relationship and dealings with God, I find some of His ways to be delightfully childlike. Maybe that's why He says we should be like little children. Perhaps that is an aspect of His likeness that He wants us to emulate. I'm convinced He is the original inventor of the game hide-and-go-seek. God takes pleasure in hiding things and then watching gleefully as we find them. I'm even more convinced of this when I come across a verse like Ephesians 3:8 which speaks of "the unsearchable riches of Christ." That short phrase is pregnant with possibilities. Think of it... unsearchable riches! Words like "unsearchable" or "unfathomable" as some translations use, give us a clue as to what is available to us in Christ. Paul, in the NET rendering of the same verse says:

Ephesians 3:8
To me—less than the least of all the saints—this grace was given, to proclaim to the Gentiles the unfathomable riches of Christ.

This is remarkable! He says that these unfathomable riches are so wondrous, it even takes grace to talk about them!

I'm intrigued by that word unfathomable because it adds another dimension of possibility. Now the word fathom comes from an Old English word meaning "outstretched arms." It was a term of measurement whereby a person would stand with his arms outstretched from side to side. The distance from the fingertip on one outstretched arm to the fingertip on the other outstretched arm was considered a fathom. It also meant to encircle something with your arms. Consequently, it became synonymous with "embrace." Later on, it was (and to a large degree still is) used as a nautical term referring to the depth of something. So, within that one word, you have a picture of the all-encompassing grace that is found in Jesus Christ. It would have been amazing if the verse had referred us to the fathomable riches of Christ. But, we are elevated to a greater level of understanding because it speaks of the unfathomable riches of Christ. That lets us know that this grace we're talking about cannot possibly be exhausted or outgrown.

I am amazed at how quickly our children grow. They go to bed and sometimes literally wake up taller. Or, before they can break in a pair of new shoes properly, there's already need for another pair. They are growing which is a wonderful thing. The only issue with their growth is that they quickly exhaust that which they are growing into. God's grace is not this way. It is unsearchable, unfathomable and inexhaustible. You cannot grow so much that you outgrow grace. In 2 Peter 3:8, we are encouraged and invited to "grow in grace and in the knowledge of our Lord and Saviour Jesus Christ." It is not possible to get access to more grace than has already been made available to you in Christ. But, you can grow in grace by attraction, impartation, and revelation. Let me show you how this works.

Grace by Attraction

God enjoys giving good gifts to His children because He is a good and loving God. With all the power He has, He could have chosen to use a tiny fraction of that power to force us into relationship with Him. Instead, He chose to draw us to himself through His love and His goodness toward us. The Bible tells us in Romans 5:8 that even while we were still sinners, God commended or demonstrated His love toward us.

Romans 5:8
But God commendeth His love toward us, in that, while we were yet sinners, Christ died for us.

God never waited for you to become good on your own, He knew it was never going to happen. But while we were yet sinners, Christ loved us and died for us. That's a hallelujah moment right there! In our evil-doing, God demonstrated His unconditional love. The only problem we have in the Church nowadays is that we have preachers who are trying to demonstrate the punishment of God to a generation that is dying in sin when it is only the unconditional love and grace of God that will save them.

Romans 2:4
The goodness of God leads you to repentance

In the Greek, the word which is rendered leads in Romans 2:4 is the word ágō which means to induce. The best way to explain the meaning of this word is to think of how a woman is induced in the birthing process. When a woman is being medically induced in labour, she is given medication in order to lessen the pain of the birthing process. While she is under the influence of that which was given to induce labour, there is no real effort on her part to stimulate birth. Being induced does not create the baby, the baby is already there. Rather, it leads the woman into the birth by stimulating contractions which cause the baby to be drawn from where it is and be delivered to the mother. As long as that baby remains where it is in the womb, the mother cannot experience the full joy of that baby being delivered and placed in her arms.

In a similar way, there is an ability in the Word of God to induce you to repentance. When you are induced by the Word, you are under the influence of the Word. That in and of itself does not produce grace. Like the baby already in the womb, grace is already there. But as you allow yourself to be influenced by the Word, it stimulates humility, and it is that humility which attracts grace, drawing it from where it already exists, and causing it to be delivered to you in a way you can fully enjoy. James 4:6 put it this way:

But He gives more grace. Therefore, He says: "God resists the proud, but gives grace to the humble."

Being induced by the Word requires no real effort on your part. Just being under the influence of the Word stimulates that humility which causes grace to be drawn to you. That is one of the ways you can grow in grace. And here is another one.

Grace by Impartation

People are different. Mike Murdock, one of the greatest students and teachers of wisdom, says that wisdom is the ability to recognize difference in people. In our way of speaking, we say that some people "carry" more grace than others. That is not to say that there are some believers who have been given abundance of grace and others who have not. According to Romans 5:17, we have all been given abundance of grace. What we mean is that there are some believers who have received from that abundance levels of grace that others have not yet received. That is why a prophet, for example, who has received grace to be a prophet, can impart to others that prophetic grace which he has already received. You cannot give what you have not received. It is your responsibility as a believer to see to it that the grace of God upon your life increases in greater measure. One of the ways you can do that is to find and receive from those who are operating in greater measures of grace than you are.

Paul in several places in the scripture would say, "Grace be unto you." These were not just nice sounding words that Paul was speaking. Paul was aware of what he carried. He knew that he could impart a greater measure of grace to you just by speaking the words, "Grace be unto you." (This is something to remember the next time a man or woman of God says, "God bless you.") As you expose yourself to the words and teachings of those who are functioning in greater measures of grace than you currently are, more grace can be imparted to you. Doesn't the Word tell you that faith comes by hearing and hearing by the word of God? Yes, it does. And that faith is a gift of grace. So, if faith, which is a gift of grace, can be imparted to you by hearing words, in a similar manner, words delivered to you by those carrying greater grace can also impart greater grace to you.

Paul also understood that grace could be imparted by proximity or by the laying on of hands.

Romans 1:11
For I long to see you, that I may impart to you some spiritual gift, so that you may be established.

Paul was in a different location from the church at Rome. He wanted to be physically close to where they were so that he could impart or give to them some spiritual gift. Paul tells Timothy:

1 Timothy 4:14
Do not neglect the gift that is in you, which was given to you by prophecy with the laying on of the hands of the eldership.

This is yet another example of grace in the form of a spiritual gift that was imparted or given. And this is not a concept that started with New Testament believers.

Moses was a man who had received great grace. The Bible tells us that God took of the Spirit that was on Moses and gave it to seventy of his elders so that they could assist him with the work he needed to accomplish (see Numbers 11:16-30). In another place, it is said of Joshua that he was full of the spirit of wisdom because Moses had laid hands on him (Deuteronomy 34:9). Moses, the one who had received greater grace, was able to impart that grace to others. Listen to what Hebrews 7:7 (AMPC) says:

Yet it is beyond all contradiction that it is the lesser person who is blessed by the greater one.

This does not mean that as a believer you are inferior to anyone. As a child of God, you have the same inheritance as every other child of God. There is a difference between what is given and what is received. What Hebrews 7:7 means is that the grace that one child of God has received may be greater than what another child of God has received, and it is the one with greater grace who is able to impart to the one who has received (or understood and taken advantage of) lesser grace. Now, let us look at another way you can grow in grace: by revelation.

Grace by Revelation

Remember, I started out this chapter by saying that God takes pleasure in hiding treasure. Proverbs 25:2 puts it this way:

It is the glory of God to conceal a thing; but the glory of kings is to search out a thing.

You can grow in grace by discovery or an unveiling of truth. It's like a treasure hunt.

I remember taking our youngest son on a treasure hunt. There were children running around a field searching every possible place for the goodies they knew were hidden there. They left no stone unturned! As long as they knew there was something else to be found, they kept on looking. And, oh the joy when a treasure was found! With each new discovery, the children would jump up and down with glee and then, with renewed motivation for discovering yet another treasure, they would set off again looking for more. Sometimes, they would even go back to the same places where they had looked before and find something that was hidden there that they had not discovered before. The joy of the one who had hidden those goodies was in knowing that children would search for and discover them. The joy of the children was to search for and find them. This is just like God. He has hidden goodies, wonderful treasures in Christ. And His joy, as well as ours, comes when we search for and discover more about Christ. Each discovery of the person of Jesus Christ is a discovery of another one of the goodies of grace.

Grace is not a muscle that you have to work out in order for it to grow. Grace does not grow. You grow in grace as you grow in the Word. And remember, in John 1 we are told that Jesus is the Word. In Galatians 4:19, Paul expressed his earnest desire for Christ to be fully formed in you. It was such a strong and forceful desire that he refers to it as birth pains. What was he saying? How is it possible for Christ, who is the Word, to be fully formed in you? 2 Peter 1:2 tells us how. It says:

Grace and peace be multiplied to you in the knowledge of God and of Jesus our Lord

Grace can be multiplied in your life through the knowledge of God and the Lord Jesus. As the knowledge of God and His Word increases in your life, you'll walk in increased grace. Christ must get bigger in you in the sense that you grow in the knowledge of who Jesus is. This knowledge we are speaking of does not come by way of scientific discovery. The word for knowledge here is the word epígnosis which means full, correct, and precise knowledge. It transcends mere awareness and mental assent and brings you into an arena of understanding. It is revelation knowledge and not everybody has it. This is exactly why there are Bible scholars who can teach and preach the word who have scientific knowledge of the Word—knowledge that is gained through their own mental activity—yet they have no revelation. Sleight of hand preachers are a good example of this. They know by mental assent what the Word says, but they lack revelation about what it means. As a result, they misapply the Word teaching and preaching the letter of it without communicating the spirit of it which can only be understood by revelation.

How I communicate about someone I have observed is completely different from how I communicate about someone who I know personally and with whom I have a relationship. The knowledge we are talking about in 2 Peter 1:2 is revelation knowledge that brings the knower into a relationship with that which is known. It is revelation knowledge that changes your life because it brings you into deeper relationship with Jesus, the ultimate hidden treasure in whom all other treasures are to be found. For Him to be known, He must be revealed by the Spirit of God. There are times when you will look into the Word at something you've seen or read before, and the Holy Spirit will give you a brand new revelation of something that had been hidden to you before. Each new revelation about Him is a revelation of grace. You don't have to search for grace. Search for, recognize, perceive, and become fully acquainted with God and His living Word, Jesus Christ and the Holy Spirit will see to it that you find all the goodies of His grace which are in Him, and you'll walk in ever-increasing grace.

Chapter Seven

Grace is not a License to Sin

Many people are only aware of the Ten Commandments, and even those who are aware would be hard-pressed to tell what each of those commandments is. There are in fact 613 commandments or laws given in the Old Testament. Imagine trying to keep that many commandments every single day. It is a struggle even to keep the Ten! So why would a good God give us laws that He knows we cannot keep? Romans 3:19-20 tells us:

Now we know that whatever the law says, it says to those who are under the law, that every mouth may be stopped, and all the world may become guilty before God. Therefore by the deeds of the law no flesh will be justified in His sight, for by the law is the knowledge of sin.

When God introduced the law, He was pointing to man's need for the Saviour. Paul tells us that whatever the law says, it is there to stop every mouth and that all the world may become guilty. Let me break it down for you. If you were sitting in a dark room, everything in there would seem clean, but the moment you open the curtains to let some light through even slightly, the dust particles in that room would be exposed by the light. Now that is not to say that the light introduced dust in the room, it just exposed the dust that you could not see in the dark.

So then, when God introduced the law, He was exposing the wickedness that was already in man and his need for the Saviour. Okay, let me break it down a bit further. Do you know why the Bible says thou shalt not steal? It is because left to your own devices you are a master crook. It doesn't say do not learn to steal, it just says don't do it because you can.

When the law that says do not lie came into place, it just exposed the fact that you are a liar. Sin needs the law in order to be sin. This is why the Bible says that the power or strength of sin is the law.

1 Corinthians 15:56
The sting of death is sin; and the strength of sin is the law.

Take traffic laws for example. If I am driving my car and fail to stop for a red light, I have committed a road traffic offence. I have broken a traffic law, not because I'm driving, and not because I failed to stop for a red light, but because there is a law that says I must stop when that traffic light is showing red. If that law did not exist, there would be nothing for me to violate.

The law makes you sin conscious, but the law does not stop you or empower you to stop sinning. On the contrary, the law will keep you trapped in a cycle of guilt, condemnation, and failure. So, whoever has been hammering you with the law has actually been pushing you further into sin. God never gave the law to stop people from sinning. He introduced the law so that people would know that they are sinners and they need salvation.

In the Jewish culture, the reason Jesus would often clash with the Pharisees and the Sadducees is that they actually thought that they had it together. They believed they could keep every single precept of the law, so they would use it to oppress the general population. Yet the truth is even when they were on their best behaviour, they were still as guilty of breaking the law as everybody else. For you to keep the law, you had to make sure that you have kept all 613 commandments, and if you broke even one, it meant that you were now guilty of breaking all 613. Honestly, there was no point in even trying!

James 2:10
For whoever shall keep the whole law, and yet stumble in one point, he is guilty of all.

Thankfully, there is a solution to the problem. Yes, 1 Corinthians 15:56 tells us that the law is the strength of sin, but the answer is found in the very next verse:

1 Corinthians 15:57
But thanks be to God, who gives us the victory through our Lord Jesus Christ.

Through Christ, we have victory over the condemnation of the law.

You're Fired!

Jesus Christ is the answer to the law problem. John 1:17 says:
For the law was given through Moses, but grace and truth came through Jesus Christ.

What you need to be victorious over sin is not the law, but grace and truth. You see, because of Christ, you are no longer under the Old Testament law, but under grace. The Old Testament law has been abolished. Ephesians 2:14-17 says:

For He Himself is our peace, who has made both one, and has broken down the middle wall of separation, having abolished in His flesh the enmity, that is, the law of commandments contained in ordinances, so as to create in Himself one new man from the two, thus making peace, and that He might reconcile them both to God in one body through the cross, thereby putting to death the enmity. And He came and preached peace to you who were afar off and to those who were near.

Just to make sure you didn't miss that, let me highlight verse 15 where it tells us that Jesus "abolished in His flesh the enmity, that is, the law of commandments contained in ordinances." Jesus abolished the Old Testament law of commandments. If the power of sin is the law, and the law has been abolished, what happens to the power of sin? There is none! When grace and truth through Jesus Christ enters the picture, sin loses its power!

That word abolish leaves no wiggle room. It means to put an end to, do away with, to render inactive, inoperative, and my personal favourite, it means unemployed! In the Old Testament, the law had a job. It was employed to teach us how utterly hopeless it was for us to try to be right with God by keeping the law and how desperately we needed Jesus. Paul in Galatians 3:24 puts it this way:

Therefore, the law was our tutor to bring us to Christ, that we might be justified by faith.

I wish I had more time to deal with that word tutor. Other translations render the word schoolmaster, or disciplinarian, or trainer. It carries with it the idea stern censorship, chastisement, and the enforcement of strict discipline. That's what the law does. The law was employed for one purpose, to make us conscious of sin. Look at what Paul says in Romans 7:7 (AMPC):

What then do we conclude? Is the Law identical with sin? Certainly not! Nevertheless, if it had not been for the Law, I should not have recognized sin or have known its meaning. [For instance] I would not have known about covetousness [would have had no consciousness of sin or sense of guilt] if the Law had not [repeatedly] said, you shall not covet and have an evil desire [for one thing and another].

The law is like a police officer whose job it is to catch you doing wrong and make sure that you know you were doing wrong. But if the law is done away with, as it has been according to what we read in Ephesians 2:15, then sin no longer has the power to work, and is therefore unemployed. Sin is not eligible for disability or workmen's liability insurance, or workmen's compensation. It can no longer earn the wages called death (see Romans 6:23).

Popular television show producer Mark Burnett created a blockbuster series called The Apprentice. The season would start off with 16 contestants. In each show, there would be a series of challenges in which the contestants had to compete.

During each episode, the host of the show would eliminate those contestants who failed the challenge. Only the fiercest competitors would make it to the next episode. Each episode would end with the host declaring what became the trademark phrase for the show, "You're fired!" By the end of the final episode, there would be only one contestant left standing who would be declared the winner.

Long before Mark Burnett conceived the idea for the show, God the Father created and hosted His own version of The Apprentice. In His version of the show, there were 616 contestants. On one team, there were the 613 commandments of the law and sin itself, and the sole contestant on the other team was the Lord Jesus Christ. One by one, each of the 613 commandments was eliminated as Christ met and conquered each challenge until only sin and Jesus were left standing. There was one final challenge, the cross. Jesus and sin both went to the cross. It was a gruelling gruesome challenge with each contestant giving their all. Sin was left hanging on the cross, Jesus died on the cross and was buried, and it looked like there wouldn't be a winner. One day passed and it looked like there would be no winner. The second day passed, and still no winner could be declared. But on the third day, Jesus was raised from the dead victorious! He looked at sin still hanging on the cross. The Father said, "Son, You do the honours." Jesus smiled triumphantly, looked at sin on the cross, and boldly declared the infamous words, "You're fired!" Hallelujah!

The Nature of God

Jesus rendered the law inoperable and dealt with sin on the cross once and for all time. We no longer have the law, we have

Jesus. Sin is no longer an issue for the born again believer because sin has been rendered powerless. 1 John 3:8 says it this way:

He who sins is of the devil, for the devil has sinned from the beginning. For this purpose the Son of God was manifested, that He might destroy the works of the devil.

Sin is the work of the devil, and that work has been destroyed by the Lord Jesus Christ. We do not sin, and we are no longer under the power of sin. I know some of you are pondering the question, what do you mean we do not sin? Let me address that by asking you a series of questions. First, do chickens bark? Go ahead, I'll give you a minute to answer. Okay, next question. Do dogs cluck? Here's another one, do pigs fly (on their own)? The answer to each of these questions is an emphatic 'No!' The question now is, why doesn't a chicken bark or a dog cluck or a pig fly (on its own)? The answer is, it's not their nature to do so.

Now, let's carry that line of thinking over to one last question. Does the new man in Christ—the born again believer—sin? Let's look to the Word in 1 John 3:9 to find the answer:

Whoever has been born of God does not sin, for His seed remains in him; and he cannot sin, because he has been born of God.

Wow! That's strong language: "does not sin" and furthermore, "cannot sin." And we're not left hanging as to the reason why. It says, "because he [or she] has been born of God." When you take the time to think about it, this answer should be no more puzzling to you than the answers to the previous questions about dogs, chickens, or pigs. The born again believer does not sin because it is not his or her nature to sin. You have been born of God, you have His nature, and His nature does not sin.

When we preach the good news of God's grace, we are awakening you to the divine nature of God that is in you that cannot sin. This new nature is evidence of the grace of God given to us. 2 Peter 1:3-4 tells us:

As His divine power has given to us all things that pertain to life and godliness, through the knowledge of Him who called us by glory and virtue, by which have been given to us exceedingly great and precious promises, that through these you may be partakers of the divine nature, having escaped the corruption that is in the world through lust.

You are a partaker of God's divine nature, and that nature does not sin. You did not do anything to earn it. You don't have to. It's a gift of His grace. Romans 8:1-3 says:

There is therefore now no condemnation to them which are in Christ Jesus, who walk not after the flesh, but after the Spirit. For the law of the Spirit of life in Christ Jesus hath made me free from the law of sin and death. For what the law could not do, in that it was weak through the flesh, God sending his own Son in the likeness of sinful flesh, and for sin, condemned sin in the flesh

Jesus has dealt with the sin issue and has introduced a greater law called the law of the Spirit of life. This greater law frees us from sin and its penalty. Instead of sin condemning you, Jesus turned it around and condemned sin for you. That's why Paul could boldly say that there is no more condemnation because of sin for you as a born again believer.

Empowered by Grace

Now that we know that the sin issue is dealt with and that condemnation is no longer a concern, does that mean that you have a license to sin? Grace does not mean that you can do anything you want. Paul addressed this concern in Romans 6:1-2 where the scripture says:

What shall we say then? Shall we continue in sin that grace may abound? Certainly not! How shall we who died to sin live any longer in it?

In case you missed it, the answer to the question of whether grace grants you a license to sin is, "Certainly not!" I like the way the King James translation puts that exclamation as "God forbid!" Grace does not encourage or in any way justify a sinful lifestyle. On the contrary, grace encourages holy living not as a way to become righteous, but as a result of righteousness.

When you understand the grace of God, it does not motivate you to sin, it motivates you to love and because of that love, you will naturally (according to your divine nature) not sin. Andrew Wommack aptly stated, "When we clearly see the grace God has extended to us, the love of God will abound in our lives and we will live more holy lives accidentally than we ever have before on purpose."

Contrary to what some anti-grace sleight of hand teachers believe, grace does not give us a license to sin. Instead, it liberates us from the dominion of sin. Romans 6:14 clearly tells us:

For sin shall not have dominion over you, for you are not under law but under grace.

Grace is an empowerment over sin. Grace strips the power of sin and grants us the power to rule over sin. We have already looked at the scripture which tells us that the strength or power of sin is the law. But the law has been replaced by grace and sin no longer has any power. Sin does not have dominion over the believer because the law has been abolished. If a person refuses to believe that and chooses instead to live by the law, then the converse is also true: sin will rule that person's life.

John 8:3-11 is a powerful demonstration of grace in action. Most of you are familiar with this passage but I want to point out a few things in there you might not have noticed. It is the account of the woman who was caught in the act of adultery. It is an illustrated sermon of all that we have talked about so far in this chapter concerning this wonderful message of grace. Let's quickly review the story together.

John 8:3-11
And the scribes and Pharisees brought unto Him a woman taken in adultery; and when they had set her in the midst, 4 They say unto him, Master, this woman was taken in adultery, in the very act. 5 Now Moses in the law commanded us, that such should be stoned: but what sayest thou? 6 This they said, tempting Him, that they might have to accuse Him.

But Jesus stooped down, and with His finger wrote on the ground, as though He heard them not. 7 So when they continued asking Him, He lifted up himself, and said unto them, He that is without sin among you, let him first cast a stone at her. 8 And again He stooped down, and wrote on the ground. 9 And they which heard it, being convicted by their own conscience, went out one by one, beginning at the eldest, even unto the last: and Jesus was left alone, and the woman standing in the midst. 10 When Jesus had lifted up himself, and saw none but the woman, He said unto her, Woman, where are those thine accusers? hath no man condemned thee? 11 She said, No man, Lord. And Jesus said unto her, Neither do I condemn thee: go, and sin no more.

Now, you need to understand that this woman had been caught in the very act of adultery. They had literally pulled her off of her accomplice. There was no question of her guilt, yet when the Lord Jesus refers to those that had brought her to him He says, where are your accusers? These guys were not accusers; they were eyewitnesses of the crime. An accuser is someone who is accusing of something that may or may not be true. A witness, on the other hand, can detail a first-hand account of what actually happened. That is why even in the courts of law today an eyewitness account is irrefutable.

The account begins with the scribes and the Pharisees dragging this adulterous woman to Jesus. But they didn't only bring the woman to Jesus, they also brought the law of which she was guilty. Her sin was exposed for everyone to see, including Jesus. Although she did not realize it at that time, that was actually a good thing. By exposing her to Jesus, the were exposing her to the One who is full of grace. Now, watch what happens.

The Pharisees had brought this woman to Jesus to judge and condemn her under the law, and the Bible says that the Lord stooped down and began to write with His finger on the ground. When Moses received the law, the Bible says that it had been written by the finger of God, and right there that same finger that authored the law they wanted to use to condemn this woman began to write, and one by one starting with the greatest they departed from his presence leaving him alone with this woman.

He asks her, "Woman, where are those accusers of yours? Has no one condemned you?" She said, "No one, Lord." He settles the issue of condemnation, "Neither do I condemn you, go and sin no more." Now this was more than just an instruction. This was an empowerment to not sin, a beautiful illustration of what happens when the strength of sin is removed, the issue of condemnation is dealt with, and the message of grace is received. It is the same thing when Jesus would say to a paralytic, "Take up thy bed and walk." It's an instruction that carries an empowerment to fulfil what has been spoken. The biggest problem we have in the Church today is that we are expecting the people to change without that empowerment of grace. This is why we preach the good news.

The Grace Change

The Gospel (euaggélion) means good news. Actually, it means more than that. A more precise interpretation would be the nearly-too-good-to-be-true news. The difficulty that many people have in accepting this message of grace is really their struggle with the "nearly-too-good-to-be-true news." It's hard for them to believe that sin is no longer an issue and that the law which gave strength to sin has been completely done away with. The grace of God is the heart of the Gospel. It grants, by a sovereign act of God's grace, absolute provision of all things necessary to be right with God. Any teaching that makes righteousness contingent upon what you do or don't do is not the Gospel. It is another Gospel, and the results are devastating.

I grew up in a very religious rules-oriented church. I never heard anything taught about the grace of God or any of the material that we have talked about in this book. What I remember more than anything else was a whole lot of rules. There were rules about what you could wear and what you couldn't wear. There were rules about what you could eat and what you couldn't eat. There were rules about where you could go and where you couldn't go, and if you could go to a certain place, who you could go there with.

We had rules about how to say hallelujah in church and only certain times an "Amen" in church was allowed. We were not allowed to even talk about going to a concert much less actually go to one, and so on, and so on, ad infinitum. There were lots of rules! We were taught that the purpose of those rules was to keep us from sinning. There was no talk of grace, yet that was the most carnal environment you could imagine! Think of a sin, and it was likely being done by somebody in this rules-regulated church. Why was there so much sin amongst the believers in this church? It was not because of the biblical teaching concerning grace, but because of the absence of it. Without an understanding of grace, the only motivation for right living is fear.

A grace filled environment is one in which love prevails. Fear is a poor motivator. Those of you who deal with children know this to be true. When a child obeys out of fear, as soon as the threat of punishment is out of sight or removed, wrong behaviour continues, and the heart of the child remains unchanged. I'm reminded of a story I heard a long time ago about a young boy who was attending church with his father. The father was a surly fellow, hardly ever smiling, and rarely if ever showing any real affection to his son. The son felt like nothing he ever did was good enough in his father's eyes. So, for the most part, he gave up trying and often misbehaved. This day was no different.

The child refused to stay in his seat. The father, aware that other people were watching, turned to the son and said angrily, "Sit down!" The child continued as if his father hadn't said anything, which angered the father even more. He turned to the boy and said more sternly, "I said, sit down!" The boy stopped for a moment, knowing that he was pressing the limits of his father's anger, but still refused to sit down. Now infuriated, the father leaned in close to the boy's face and threatened, "Either you sit down, or I'll take you around the back and give you such a beating you won't be able to sit down!" Knowing the father would make good on his threat, the boy stopped in his tracks and sat down. But then he looked at his father and with a glint of defiance in his eyes he said, "I may be sitting down, but in my heart, I'm still standing up!"

This is a picture of what is happening in many churches all over the world where the message of grace is not properly taught. People either go through the motions of doing what they are being told to do, or they stop trying altogether because they feel they can't please God anyway. They see God as this menacing giant waiting for them to slip up so He can punish them. If out of fear they try to do what they think God wants them to do, their hearts remain unchanged, just like the little boy. But an unchanged heart is not what grace produces.

The revelation of grace changes everything. Grace is the greatest motivation for right living, not a license to sin. I believe the woman who had been caught in the act of adultery left the presence of Jesus with a changed heart because she had experienced the liberty of grace. In all probability, this woman was familiar with the law and knew that adultery carried a penalty of death. Yet, knowing this law and the penalty did not stop her from sinning. Understanding the revelation of grace eclipses any desire to sin. Grace produces right living, not because you're afraid of what will happen if you were to sin, but because you love this God who has lavished so much grace on you.

Chapter Eight

Falling from Grace

Now when we talk about falling from grace, I know a lot of things come to mind. For instance, that preacher who used to be so powerful but got caught up in some scandal, now there is not much left to say of him. That is actually not what we are talking about here, and I know there are a lot of misconceptions on the matter. It is a lot simpler than what you think. Let's get in the Word.

Galatians 1:6
I marvel that ye are so soon removed from Him that called you into the grace of Christ unto another gospel.

There are people out there that can remove you from the grace of Christ through their religious doctrines that are not even biblical. When we are talking about falling from grace, it is that very act of turning away or being removed from the grace of Christ and going back into living by the law. Imagine the joy you felt when you first got born again, the freedom you enjoyed. You were a sinner and you knew it, but the joy came when you realised that Christ loves you just as you are. But now that you have been in church long enough to learn the do's and don'ts, that weight of sin is pulling you down again.

Even when the worship leader says let's lift up holy hands, the enemy whispers, are those really holy hands, and you hesitate and even cower from worshipping God. That, brothers and sisters, is falling from grace. When you are no longer standing on what Christ has done as your foundation but relying on your own works, you can be removed from the grace of Christ. That means you will not be able to take advantage of what Christ has done and the enemy will have a field day with you.

Believers actually have an ability to nullify everything that God had done through the sacrifice of Christ. Yes, you heard me right. You can actually void the power and authority of God's Word in your own life when you fail to renew your mind to the truth of God's Word. Right now, half of the things that are taught and done in church are not done or taught that way because that is what the Word of God says but because we have always done it that way. We have become a church of traditions and not a church of the Word. Even if you think back to the things you were learning in Sunday School as a kid, there is a Bible verse for it.

Okay, let me give you an example. How many funerals have you gone to where the preacher will say, the Lord gives, and the Lord has taken away? Yet the Bible says that it is the thief that comes to kill, steal and destroy. Check your Bible, every time Jesus would attend a funeral, He would turn the whole thing on its head. Yet because of tradition, you unwittingly adopt things that are not even biblical, and they rob the Church of power and authority. Watch what the Bible says:

Mark 7:13
Making the word of God of none effect through your tradition, which ye have delivered: and many such like things do ye.

The reason why the message of grace is fought so viciously in Christian circles is that it's not the way we have always done things or understood things, so immediately the conclusion is, there must be something wrong with what we are hearing.

It reminds me of when slaves in America were declared free. There were slaves who did not want to be free. When presented with the opportunity for freedom versus slavery, they chose to remain where they were in a life of servitude. Some slaves were free and did not know they were free. As a result, they never experienced the joys of their newfound liberty. Other slaves received the news of their freedom with joy and left their slave masters only to later return to a life of bondage. They had grown accustomed to hard labour, and getting by with barely enough, and trying to please the master. Freedom was a new and foreign concept for which they had no frame of reference, and the possibilities frightened rather than empowered them. They found it difficult to imagine a life where they didn't have to strive and work and labour under a hard taskmaster. They said to themselves, "We've never done it that way before." So, they returned to the familiarity of bondage.

Just like the various ways slaves responded to their freedom, there are various ways people respond to the gift of grace. Grace was designed to bring us into a life of liberty. You have been declared free by God's grace through faith in Jesus Christ. Yet there are those who reject the gift of grace in its entirety and choose to never be free. There are others who receive salvation by grace, but they do not really know how to maximize the benefits of grace. And then there are others who also receive salvation by grace, but afterward, return to the bondage of performance-based righteousness. It is the latter scenario that we will deal with primarily in this chapter. Like the mindset of slaves that rebelled against the prospects of freedom, there are some in the Church who would rather cling to a familiar works-based religious ideology as opposed to embracing the liberty that grace brings.

The price of liberty was not cheap. In Galatians 3:13, the Bible tells us:

Christ has redeemed us from the curse of the law, having become a curse for us (for it is written, "Cursed is everyone who hangs on a tree")

The cross shows us that Jesus paid it all. He took our sins into His own body on the tree. If you truly get an understanding of the cross, it should lead you to relate to God on the basis of His grace and not your works. A person caught up in legalism—works-based religion—has missed the message of the cross, and that message is that Jesus paid it all! Hallelujah! That's the good news!

He did not put His grace on layaway and turn the remainder of the payments over to you. He paid the price in full so that His grace would be fully available to you. We could not pay our own debt. Jesus came and did what He did because we were completely incompetent and incapable of being made right with God on our own. No religious act on our part could compensate for our sins. That is why whenever believers return to legalism, they forsake the message of the cross and shift away from grace.

You Can't Have It Both Ways

Paul is a man who knew all about trying to be good enough through religious acts. Before His personal encounter with Jesus, he was a member of the Pharisees who demanded the strictest obedience to every Jewish law and custom. He lived a good portion of his life trying to be righteous through his own good works. But everything changed after he experienced the grace of the Lord Jesus Christ. By revelation, He discovered that when you try to be justified by your own works, Christ and all He accomplished becomes of no effect to you. In Galatians 3:2, Paul puts it this way:

Indeed I, Paul, say to you that if you become circumcised, Christ will profit you nothing.

Now I need you to understand something right here. Paul was actually telling them that when you choose to make fulfilling the law your primary focus, you can no longer benefit from what Christ has done for you. You actually make the cross of Christ of non-effect by following the law and traditions of the Jews.

He was telling you that living by the law is living as though Christ died for nothing. Remember, Paul was a Jew. The Living Bible translates Paul's own description of himself as "a real Jew if there ever was one!" Paul used to live strictly by the law. So, when he talked about living life by the law and about circumcision, which was a rite of the law, he knew exactly what he was talking about. In this particular passage, circumcision wasn't really the issue being dealt with. It was just an issue that the church at Galatia was dealing with at that particular time.

The real issue that is being addressed is putting faith in actions instead of putting faith in Christ. And that issue is still very relevant today.

If a person is trusting in some act of their own holiness to make them right with God, then they've missed grace. Right actions are a by-product not a means of getting right with God. There is only one way to get right with God, and that is by grace through faith in the Lord Jesus Christ. How can you know if you're putting faith in your own actions? Here is an easy way to test. If the Lord was to look at you and ask you what makes you worthy to enter Heaven what would your answer be? Whatever comes to your heart is what your trust is in. If you point to anything you've done right or well, or if you point at anything except the Saviour, you would never make it in. This is what Paul means when he speaks of Christ profiting you nothing. Your only claim to enter Heaven is Jesus as your Lord and Saviour. Good works and faith in them have nothing to do with it.

What does your life as a believer look like? What are the results of Christ being in your life? If you're struggling like everyone else, suffering like everyone else, and you can't see the results of Christ being in your life, Christ is not profiting you the way He's supposed to. And if you're not seeing the results of Christ profiting you, it is likely because you are trusting in your own actions. Make no mistake about it, it's good to do the right things, but your faith cannot be in those things. If you put your trust in your own works, you will have to keep the entire law in order to be right with God. And if that's the case, even if you miss one point of the law, you will lose everything. Nobody could ever fulfil every requirement of the law other than the

Lord Jesus Christ. The only way you will ever be able to obtain peace with God and be right with Him is by putting faith in what Jesus has done and accepting peace with God as a gift of His grace.

Good without God

The biggest problem that the Lord had with the Pharisees was not that they were the biggest lawbreakers in the land, but that they put their trust in their belief that they could outperform everyone else in terms of keeping the law. What they did not understand as many today is that you cannot be good without God. He actually considers it as a great evil for you to even try to do it without Him. When the Galatians were falling into the same trap, Paul called it witchcraft.

Galatians 3:1-3
O foolish Galatians, who hath bewitched you, that ye should not obey the truth, before whose eyes Jesus Christ hath been evidently set forth, crucified among you? This only would I learn of you, Received ye the Spirit by the works of the law, or by the hearing of faith? Are ye so foolish? having begun in the Spirit, are ye now made perfect by the flesh?

We have witchcraft in the church today, people trying to outperform God. And when you look at it from the outside, it actually seems as if those that are preaching the law are doing such a noble thing. It is when you get close and see the results that you see the error. This exactly what Paul was trying to warn Timothy about in his letter.

2 Timothy 3:5
Having a form of godliness, but denying the power thereof: from such turn away.

It is having an appearance of a godly person, yet all you are doing is just coming out of your human effort, and God is not in the equation. As I said before, doing good things is a good thing. The problem comes in when you do good things to be right with God. A person who is trying to do good to be right with God is always going to fall short. This is the issue with trying to be justified by the law. Romans 11:6 (ERV) says:

And if He chose them by grace, then it is not what they have done that made them His people. If they could be made His people by what they did, His gift of grace would not really be a gift.

That verse speaks for itself. You cannot earn your relationship with God. If you could, Christ would be of no effect to you and as the verse says, "His gift of grace would not really be a gift." You are saved by grace through faith plus nothing else. You can't put total faith in Jesus and total faith in your own actions or good works too. It's one or the other. You either have to put your faith in God's grace and trust Jesus and what He's done or trust yourself and what you've done, but you can't have it both ways.

Finish the Way You Started

You cannot live the Christian life in your own strength. You can't be good enough or holy enough. The only way this grace driven life will work is if you are totally dependent on what Christ has done for you. It is His life flowing through you that makes you holy. It is not holiness that makes His life flow through you. And there's a big difference. That difference is the difference between victory and defeat, joy and peace versus frustration. The person who is trying to live good enough will be frustrated, and will not have victory, joy, or peace. But the person who has learned to appropriate by faith the grace given to you in Christ will experience God's life flowing through them and they will live holy without even trying.

For those of you who think that you are not doing enough to merit the grace of God, ask yourself, what were you doing before you got born again? How much tithing were you doing? How much praying and fasting were you doing? Probably none of the above! Most people were not religious at all before they were born again. They didn't pray three times a day. They weren't baptized by immersion. They didn't talk right, act right, or live right. They didn't do any of those things, and yet they qualified to receive salvation as a gift, not based on what they were or were not doing. Why is it then that after being saved, those same people think that they have to work to keep the salvation they received as a gift? That just doesn't make good sense.

Righteousness is a gift. Faith is a gift. Grace is a gift. Salvation is a gift. If you do something to get a gift, it's no longer a gift, it's a wage.

Colossians 2:6
As you therefore have received Christ Jesus the Lord, so walk in Him.

That means, if you didn't work to get Him, don't try to work to keep Him. If you entered into relationship with Him by grace, maintain that relationship by the same grace. The same way you received salvation is the same way you should continue to walk in salvation. If you are truly born again, you were born again by grace and putting faith in God's grace not by something you did to earn it.

There's a saying that goes, "You have to catch a fish before you clean it." It's a phrase I've often heard preachers use in the context of evangelism. What they are communicating is that anyone can (or should be able to) walk into a church even in their worst condition and have the opportunity to have salvation ministered to them by grace. In other words, you don't try to clean them up before salvation. I've often heard people say they know they need to be born again, but they want to get themselves together first. That's not the way it works at all. Jesus said, I didn't come to invite good people to turn to God. I came to invite sinners (Luke 5:32 CEV). Jesus did not come to make salvation conditional on you cleaning up and getting it all together first. He offers His grace to you just as you are. Once you have received Jesus by grace, you need to continue to relate to Him on the basis of grace.

I'm staying on this point because I want to make sure you get it. You don't have to try and earn something that has already been offered as a gift. God is not going to respond to your goodness or your holiness. You have to receive it as a gift or do without. Unfortunately, most believers are doing without. This does not mean that they're not born again. But it does mean that the victory, peace, and joy they should have as grace driven believers will be suffocated by the frustration, guilt, and condemnation of a works-based life. If being born again was all about legalistic dos and don'ts, what would make Christianity different from any other religion? There would be no distinction. It is grace and faith in what Jesus has done that makes the difference. It is Jesus and your faith in Him that makes you accepted. Making a religious system out of Christianity instead of total dependence on Christ is falling from grace. And this applies to every believer.

Sometimes we make the mistake of thinking that falling from grace only applies to the pew members and not those in the pulpit, you know, the really anointed ones. Of course, I'm being a bit facetious. Every believer is anointed. Some function in greater levels of the anointing than others. But, the point is that God has never had anyone qualified working for Him. That is why we use the expression, God does not call the qualified, He qualifies the called. There are a lot of anointed people in ministry who think that just because God works through them to perform miracles, signs, and wonders that gives them a leg up on being right with God. No sir! Any anointed person, from the pulpit to the back door, who relies on their anointing or any other work to get them on God's A-list, they too have fallen from grace.

Fake Falling

It is very important to understand what falling from grace is and is not. Some people think it means falling from a level of success, but it is actually falling into law from a position of grace. Some make the mistake of thinking they have fallen from grace, when in reality, they were never there. Let me give you a couple examples to explain what I mean.

There is something in the UK referred to as common law marriage or common law spouses where two people live together for some time as though they are married. However, in the eyes of the law, a common law marriage is not recognized as a legal status with the same rights and responsibilities. In short, they do not have the same legal rights as married couples. It is not much more than a social partnership and a "marriage" in name only. In such a scenario, if such a couple wanted to divorce, it would be impossible. There is no legal union or marriage to dissolve because they were never in a legal marriage. They could not fall from marriage into divorce because they were never in a marriage.

Let me give another quick example before I make my point. Let's say I think I've fallen off a ladder. If I've never climbed up a ladder, it would not be possible for me to fall from the ladder because I was never up there. The only way I can fall from a ladder is for me to be up on the ladder at some point. I'm using common law marriage and falling from ladders as examples to illustrate an important point about falling from grace. The point is, you cannot fall from a place where you have never been. Let me explain further.

If a church is preaching the law—that is to say, using works to justify being right with God—and that is all they've ever preached, they haven't fallen from grace. They were never there to begin with. Falling from grace means to begin from a position of grace and then go back under the law as a means of being right with God. This is what the passage in Hebrews 6:4-6 is talking about:

For it is impossible for those who were once enlightened, and have tasted the heavenly gift, and have become partakers of the Holy Spirit, and have tasted the good word of God and the powers of the age to come, if they fall away, to renew them again to repentance, since they crucify again for themselves the Son of God, and put Him to an open shame.

You fall or shift away from grace if you started from there and then try to replace grace with something else, namely works.

Stay Free

God did not give us what I call push start or jump start grace. Those who are familiar with automobiles that use manual transmissions know that if the car won't start, you can still get the car going by putting it in gear and giving it a push to get it started. Once the car gets going, you no longer need to push. You can go on your own. A similar example is when you jump start a car with a dead battery. You can take a charged or live battery that has power, connect it to the dead battery, and power will flow from the live battery to the dead battery enabling the driver to start the car and get going. This is not what God did for you. He did not get you started and then expect you to take it from there. The power of grace that got you started has enough power to keep you going.

I recently heard a brilliant person pose the following question: when did you receive power, before or after you were born again? A few who were brave enough to respond audibly said you receive power after you're born again. Perhaps they were thinking of what it says in Acts 1:8, but it was not the right answer for that question. The answer was found in John 1:12 (KJV):

But as many as received Him, to them gave He power to become the sons of God, even to them that believe on His name.

Notice, He gave them power to become. He did not wait until they were sons of God and then give them power. It takes power to become the sons of God. Therefore, God gives you power before you become a believer and it is that power that enables you to become a believer. Did you get that? You don't become a son or daughter of God without power. You receive power first to become born again, and that same power keeps you going, not your own. This is the difference between the grace driven life and a life that is driven by the law or good works. The grace driven life depends on Christ from start to finish. When you revert back to your own works to finish, it's like you're saying to God, "Thanks for the push start, but I can take it from here."

Do you know what Paul calls that? Stupid. I'm not trying to be insulting. It's right there in Galatians 3:1-3. Let's look at it again:

Galatians 3:1-3
O foolish Galatians, who hath bewitched you, that ye should not obey the truth, before whose eyes Jesus Christ hath been evidently set forth, crucified among you? This only would I learn of you, Received ye the Spirit by the works of the law, or by the hearing of faith? Are ye so foolish? having begun in the Spirit, are ye now made perfect by the flesh?

That word "foolish" in verse 1 literally means just plain stupid! And just in case you didn't catch it the first time, Paul repeats the word in verse 3. He's saying it's just plain stupid to start off God's way and try to finish your own way.

Thankfully, God doesn't leave you stuck on stupid. A couple chapters later in Galatians 5:1, he offers this wise counsel:

Stand fast therefore in the liberty by which Christ has made us free, and do not be entangled again with a yoke of bondage. Paul here is defending grace as the means to relationship with God. To stand fast means to persevere, stand firm, to hold one's ground. What he's saying is that this liberty is not automatic. That is to say, it doesn't function without faith on our part. The very fact that he tells us to stand fast suggests that there will be people and forces that will try to move us. We have this liberty, but there are times when we have to fight, not to earn it but to defend it.

In the latter part of the verse, he cautions us to "not be entangled again with a yoke of bondage." This yoke of bondage is the Old Testament law, the system of works-based righteousness. He warns us to stay away from that. He says don't be entangled or ensnared. If you base your confidence on God accepting you on your performance, it becomes a snare to you, like a net. The more you struggle trying to be right with God, the more unworthy you feel because you're actually putting your faith in yourself and what you do in your own strength. Yokes are usually put on by others. Don't allow anyone to put a yoke of religious restraints and restrictions on you. Christ set you free to be free. Stay that way.

Stay Connected

I am not saying that if a person gets a legalistic attitude and falls into trusting in his or her own good merits for their salvation he or she is not born again. But Galatians 5:4 tells us what happens when you do this:

Some of you are trying to be made right with God by obeying the law. You have been separated from Christ. You have fallen away from God's grace.

Think about what it means to be separated or as some translations put it, severed from Christ. Jesus gives us a clue in John 15:5 (AMPC) where He says:

I am the Vine; you are the branches. Whoever lives in Me and I in him bears much (abundant) fruit. However, apart from Me [cut off from vital union with Me] you can do nothing.

To be severed from Christ means to be cut off from union with Him. This disconnection does not change the nature of the relationship. He is still the Vine and you are still the branch. But when you are cut off from Him, you function as if there is no union between the two. You can no longer benefit from the connection. When this happens, you have fallen away from God's grace. Understand that trusting in your own works to be made right with God has the opposite effect on your relationship with Him. Instead of drawing you closer to Him, it alienates you from Him. This does not mean that you're lost or damned to hell. But it does mean that you have put yourself in a place where God cannot be good to you or show you His kindness the way He wants to.

Some years ago, I visited a certain place in South Africa. I went with a team of pastors. On the night of our arrival, we gathered together to study the Word and to pray. Not long after we assembled, the Holy Spirit began to move in a marvellous way. He ministered to each of us individually about a particular area He wanted to address. For me, it was about receiving grace. You see, I was good at giving, but not so good at receiving. I had been so used to doing things on my own, that when it came to my walk with Christ, I was not allowing Him to be gracious to me the way He wanted to. When He told me this, I was filled with remorse thinking I had blown it. But He assured me that He was telling me this so that I could now begin to walk with Him in a greater revelation of grace and receive of His bountiful goodness. I have never been the same since that night.

My purpose in discussing this subject of falling from grace with you is not to frighten you or make you feel guilty or to judge you. Quite the opposite. Like the experience I had that night in South Africa, I want you to receive of His fulness. My desire for you is that you get the revelation of His grace and walk in it daily. I want you to be conscious of the fact that you don't have to strive to be right with God. If you have received His Son by faith, know that you already are. Receive of His grace and refuse to fall into the trap of a performance-based relationship with Him.

Chapter Nine

Grace as A Settled Matter

Grace is what God does for us independent of us. You don't earn it. Everything about your salvation came to you as a free gift. That is why Ephesians 2:8 (GNT) says:

For it is by God's grace that you have been saved through faith. It is not the result of your own efforts, but God's gift, so that no one can boast about it.

Neither the faith or the grace is the result of your own efforts. Both are free gifts. Some people think that we, by our faith, can move God, and manipulate Him and force Him to do things. That's equally wrong. We aren't saved by grace and we aren't saved by faith, we're saved by grace through faith.

You may be struggling with the issue of what is God's part, and what is your part. Maybe you're wondering, what does God want me to do. Let me help you with this one. He wants you to understand what He has provided. Faith is not something you do to get God to do something. Faith is your positive response to what God has already accomplished by grace. Faith is how you appropriate what God has already provided. Wonderful things happen when we stop trying to get God to do something and start believing and acting on what He has already done.

Start putting faith in grace instead of faith in what (you think) you could do to make God move. This is where a lot of people are missing it. Take healing for example. God has already made provision by His grace for you to be healed. He tells us that by the stripes of Jesus, you were already healed (see 1 Peter 2:24). Therefore, you're not the sick trying to get well. You're the well. The only issue you have to deal with is Satan trying to steal your health from you. You already have victory. You're not fighting in order to gain victory. You're already more than a conqueror. You're not trying to get there. You're already there. You don't have to try to get what you've already got. And you don't have to try to get to where you already are.

The Grace Equation

The Christian life isn't about how to get God to do anything. Yet most of us have heard some message about seven steps to get God to do this or three ways to get God to do that. People are looking for God to do something new. But God has already done everything He's going to do. Let's do a quick math lesson to illustrate this point. Don't worry! You won't have to figure anything out. I'll do like God does and provide the answers for you!

In math, there is something referred to as the transitive property of equality. Stated, it looks like this:
If $a = b$, and $b = c$, then it follows that $a = c$.

Now, the Bible says in Colossians 2:9, that the fullness of the Godhead is in Christ. Let's say that's the '$a = b$' part of our equation. The Bible also tells us in Colossians 1:27 that Christ is in you. Let's call this truth 'b = c' in our equation. Now, let's apply the transitive property of equality. If the fullness of the Godhead is in Christ (a = b) and Christ is in you (b = c), then it follows that the fullness of the Godhead is in you (a = c). While this transitive property of equality cannot be applied in every case, it certainly holds true here.

The fullness of the Godhead dwells in you bodily. That means you don't need God to do anything! In your spirit, you already have everything that exists in the fullness of the Godhead. Love, joy, peace, power, holiness, righteousness, goodness—these things are all in you because they are in God and God is in you. These aren't things that if you pray hard enough and study the Word enough and do right enough God will give you these things. In your spirit you already have these things 24 hours a day, 365 days of the year, 366 days if it's a leap year.

Don't Fight For, Defend From

If you are one of the many believers who is struggling with this truth, it's because you are living your life based on what your flesh or your feelings are telling you. What you need is a revelation of what God has already given you in your spirit. Look at it this way. Let's say I gave you a check for all the money you could ever need. If that were the case, you would not need to come and ask me for money anymore, would you? Of course not. But, let's suppose a thief came and tried to take that check away from you. I'm sure I would not be exaggerating when I say that Bruce Lee, Jackie Chan, and Jet Li would have nothing on you! You would do what you needed to do to make sure that what was given to you is not stolen from you.

In like manner, you have been given every spiritual blessing, and the enemy comes to steal what's already yours. The other strategy he uses is to convince you that you don't already have it and that you need to do something to get it. But once you know what's yours, it's much easier to defend what you've already got than to try and get something that you don't have. There are people who pray or request prayer for God to give them more love. Such a request assumes that God measured out a certain amount of love and then said, you only get this much, and if you want more you have to do something to get it. And that's just not true. Romans 5:5 tells us that God has poured out His love in our hearts by the Holy Ghost who is given to us. It does not say that He poured out some love or a little bit of love. God did not say, come into My shop and pay Me with your good works and you can buy or earn more love. He gave you the whole shop!

Grace Is Always On

Here's another thing about grace. Grace is not only independent of you, but grace is consistent. Since it's not based on you, it's not based on whether you've lived holy or on anything you've done right or wrong. It's always the same. The grace of God never fluctuates, it never changes. The grace of God is not a light switch that God switches on or off based on what you do. This is what religion teaches us. But grace is always on and in full effect.

Now I know some might be wondering, what about the verse In James 4:6 that says:

But He gives more grace. Therefore, He says: "God resists the proud, but gives grace to the humble."

Do you know what it means to be humble? To be humble does not mean you work to get more or even that you work to be humble. It simply means you open your heart to receive more of what's already been provided. Picture this. It's raining nonstop pouring down in torrents, and there are two barrels. One of the barrels has a lid on it and the other does not. So, one barrel is being continuously filled with rain, and the other is not. The rain hasn't changed. It's being supplied continuously and in abundance. The only difference is one barrel is open to receive everything and the other will require some human intervention or effort to remove the lid so that it can receive more. Which barrel are you? Will you believe and receive or doubt and do without? Realize that Christ has already removed the lid and be open to receive from the continuous downpour of God's grace!

Confusing God

Let's look quickly at Ephesians 1:3:

Blessed be the God and Father of our Lord Jesus Christ, who has blessed us with every spiritual blessing in the heavenly places in Christ

God has blessed us. It's already been done. It doesn't say God "who is going to" bless us. So much of what is called church today is religious and far removed from the Bible. It's mostly about what God is going to do and what's coming, and what you're going to get. The problem with such messages is that they imply that right now there's nothing as though God hasn't done anything yet. As one person put it, it's like God is the great I'm going to be rather than the great I Am. And yet, that is not the message from the Bible.

That's one of the wonderful things about the book of Ephesians. It's written from the standpoint of a work completed rather than a work in progress. Let's look at the verse one more time:

Blessed be the God and Father of our Lord Jesus Christ, who has blessed us with every spiritual blessing in the heavenly places in Christ.

He is not going to bless us, He has already blessed us! He has already passed those blessings out. Yet how many people pray and say, Oh God, bless me! They think they need to be blessed. The truth is, they are already blessed, they just haven't received it yet. God has already commanded the blessing upon you. Why are you asking God to do something that He's already done? That's like me handing you my Bible and then you come and ask me for the same Bible I just gave you so that you can look up a scripture. You have the Bible already, just open it up and use it! How do you respond to a person who asks you to give something that you've already given to them? If it were possible for God to be confused—and we know that's not possible, but if it were—I believe such a request would confuse even God!

In the Key of Grace

You've already been blessed! You've already got love, joy, and peace. You've already got righteousness. You don't need God to give it to you or to give you more. Yet you approach God as if

His transmitter is not working properly and requires maintenance. There's nothing wrong with His transmitter. If you don't feel righteous, it's not God who hasn't transmitted it, it's you who haven't received it. What you need to do is work on your receiving not on God's transmitting.

It's just like television signals. You can't see them, you can't hear them, but they're right there where you are. When you get a television and plug it in and turn it on and the broadcast comes on, that's not when the signal starts. The signal is already there being broadcast 24 hours a day, 7 days a week. It's not like there is a crew of cameramen and actors and other technicians waiting for you to turn on your television so a director can shout, "Action!" and then the broadcast starts. That's not the way it works. When you turn on the television, that's when you start receiving.

In Ephesians 1:15-18, we find a portion of one of the prayers of Paul the Apostle. This prayer was prayed for the saints in Ephesus and for the saints who would come two thousand years in the future and beyond. Let's read the prayer that Paul prayed together:

Ephesians 1:15-18
Therefore I also, after I heard of your faith in the Lord Jesus and your love for all the saints, do not cease to give thanks for you, making mention of you in my prayers: that the God of our Lord Jesus Christ, the Father of glory, may give to you the spirit of wisdom and revelation in the knowledge of Him, the eyes of your understanding being enlightened; that you may know what is the hope of His calling, what are the riches of the glory of His inheritance in the saints.

Look at the way Paul approaches this. Paul does not beg God to do anything. All He asks God to do is give those he was praying for a revelation of what He had already done. He didn't ask God to do anything new. He just asked God to open up their eyes. You might say, I know that I have been made righteous and I know that grace is being poured out in my life in abundance, but I don't have a revelation of it, so I've not been walking in it. What you need to do is pray for a revelation of what the Word of God says is true. That is a prayer God can respond to. That is a prayer that will fix your receiver.

Some of you may be convinced that you are trying to receive but you feel like the devil is blocking the signal. Let me ask you a question. If the all-powerful God is the transmitter, what devil do you think is powerful enough to block His signal? Do you think God has to try and try again because of anything the devil is doing? You may be thinking, what about Daniel, wasn't God's transmission (of an answered prayer) blocked? Let's settle that issue once and for all. Daniel was not a recipient of the grace you as a new creation believer have now received. Daniel was operating under a different set of rules because Jesus had not yet died, risen again, and broken the dominion of the devil. Listen to what Colossians 1:13 (AMPC) says:

[The Father] has delivered and drawn us to Himself out of the control and the dominion of darkness and has transferred us into the kingdom of the Son of His love.

He has transferred us into the kingdom of His Son and that kingdom is full of grace. That's where you live, and God did not issue you a temporary visa. Your residency in that kingdom is permanent.

Do you understand what it means to be transferred into such a kingdom? That word transferred in the Greek is methístēmi and it means to transfer, remove from one place to another, or transpose. In musical terms, transpose means to restate the notes at a different level from where it was. That's what God did for your life. He transposed you from a low key life to a high key life. You live under a new set of rules! You are no longer under the control and the dominion of the devil. Refuse to allow the lies of the enemy or any teaching or doctrine that supports those lies to play you in the wrong key. Stay in the key God set for you. Your life is a song that is meant to be played in the key of grace!

Live the Life You Dreamed About

Let me give you this last example before I wrap this up. A group of emerging entrepreneurs had gathered for a seminar that they hoped and believed would change their lives. They had big dreams but little or no capital, but they believed given the right information, they could accomplish the life they dreamed about. The speaker got up to address the group and asked the following question. What would you do if money were no object? All the nervous tension in the room seemed to disappear as the group joyfully contemplated the question. Some in the group began to mention what they would do. Others broke out in a big grin as they began to imagine the kind of life that such a reality would afford them. You could almost see lights go on in their minds as the possibilities of such a life began to open up to them.

I want you to consider that same question for a moment. What would your life look like if you had all the money you ever needed and you knew it would never run out? Do you think you would spend your life worrying about whether you had enough to live the kind of life that you dreamed about, or do you think you would wake up every day with a big grin on your face knowing that you could enjoy all the benefits of what you already knew was available to you? The answer is obviously the latter scenario.

Now I want you to apply that same line of thinking to grace instead of money and ask yourself the same question. What would you do if you knew you had all the grace you ever needed and you knew it would never run out? What would your life look like? Take a snapshot of that picture. Frame it with your imagination.

That's the life God wants you to live. God does not want you constantly worrying that every time you mess up or don't do something that you think you're supposed to do that He is angry with you or that He loves you any less. He wants you to wake up every day with a big grin on your face knowing that all of the benefits that His grace has provided are there for you to enjoy. And then He wants you to go ahead and enjoy them. His grace is sufficient for you no matter where you are in life at this point in time. Take advantage of that grace and reign as a king in this life. That, my friend, is the grace driven life that God wants you to live.

Milton Keynes UK
Ingram Content Group UK Ltd.
UKHW041846210624
444404UK00003B/5/J

9 780995 749955